THE FIRST QUARTER OF THE MOON

BY

MICHEL TREMBLAY

D1500629

TRANSLATED FROM THE FRENCH

BY

SHEILA FISCHMAN

TALONBOOKS   VANCOUVER   1994

Copyright © 1989 Leméac Éditeur
Translation copyright © 1994 Sheila Fischman

Published with the assistance of the Canada Council.

Talonbooks
201 - 1019 East Cordova
Vancouver, British Columbia
Canada V6A 1M8

Typeset in Garamond and printed and bound in Canada by Hignell Printing Ltd..

First Printing: August 1994

Le Premier Quartier de la Lune was first published in 1989 by Leméac Éditeur, Montréal, Québec.

Canadian Cataloguing in Publication Data

Tremblay, Michel, 1942-
    [Premier quartier de la lune. English]
    The first quarter of the moon

    Translation of: Le premier quartier de la lune.
    ISBN 0-88922-352-1

    I. Title. II. Title: Premier quartier de la lune. English.
PS8539.R47P7313 1994   C843'.54   C94-910661-5
PQ3919.2.T73P7313 1994

*To Chantal Beaupré, Louise Latraverse, Loui Maufette
and René Richard Cyr with all my affection.*

Whenever Victoire spotted the first quarter of the moon she'd always say: "Look at that, the good Lord's just cut off a toenail..." Me, I'd think: "The world's got off to a fresh start, like it does every twenty-eight days."

Josaphat-le-violon, in *The Sayings of Victoire*

He walked out of the house precisely at the moment when summer was beginning. A shudder in the trees, a blackout, a sigh that went to the very heart of Fabre Street, a hesitation inside of time itself, as if nature wanted to be quite sure that the fine weather had really arrived, that there would be no more fits and starts, no more hesitations, before it continued on its way; then a brief and violent silence that was more than an absence of sound, a hole. The entire city was suspended, motionless, waiting for the signal to go on living.

He told himself that nothing more existed, that he was frozen forever, that now he was part of a photograph depicting the first second of the summer of 1952, a blowup of a high-contrast black-and-white photo, as glossy as if it had just been varnished. A nine-year-old boy stood on the top step of the outside staircase of the three-storey red brick house. He was at the very centre of the picture so you couldn't make out his features, for his image was too small. But he seemed reluctant to descend the eighteen steps that led to the sidewalk. He looked straight ahead, one foot in the air: Someone had just shouted his name, or he had just witnessed something that surprised him. He was the only living being in the snapshot. There was no sign of a household pet — a bird, a cat or dog — and you might think that it was very early in the morning, that perhaps the little boy was running away. The bag he was carrying on his back, though, wasn't a runaway's bundle, but a schoolbag with straps he hadn't bothered to fasten in his eagerness to be out of the house. It was a picture that sent a shiver up your spine because you should have been able to sense some movement in it — after all, a little boy going down a staircase is full of life, he makes noise, he stirs up the air — while here, on the contrary, this immobility, so studied, almost willed, made you uncomfortable because of what was remarkable about it: There was something mysterious about that child caught in mid-movement. During the second when the picture had been snapped some mystery had occurred. This was a photograph of a mystery.

He had a brief dizzy spell but instead of bending over or leaning on the railing, he straightened up, stretched his neck and gulped some air, holding it in as long as he could. The signal came, but too soon for his liking: The tree in front of the house stirred as if a storm were coming though there was no wind and no clouds could be seen in the sky, then a bird screeched like an electric drill and the light lost some of its brilliance. The knot was undone. Around him everything was already starting again to stir, to live, to murmur; once more, it was a normal summer morning, beautiful, with greens that still moved you and the most glorious blue sky — but normal. Banal, almost. He wished the dizziness would last, wished he'd had enough time to prepare to greet the summer as it deserved, as a hero; he wished he could take the time to drink in this first second, greedily, leisurely, to taste its promises, because for two long months — all of July, all of Augus — he was going to be free to do whatever he wanted: to tell his friends endless, complicated stories, whereas now he had barely had time to breathe in this divine moment before it disappeared forever into universal memory, fixed in a photograph with the both of them as subject — he himself, and that first second of summer. Once again he felt frustrated by something he hadn't really been able to take advantage of. It lasted as long as a heartbeat: a frustrating sense of something elusive, the certainty that he was experiencing a moment that was important but beyond his reach, and then there was only himself, in the middle of the world.

He descended a few steps, sat down, his bent knees high, hands gripping the toes of his shoes, mouth pasted against a scab that was nearly dry but that his mother, the fat woman, had forbidden him to pick off. After all, he had a few minutes to spare. To imprint on his memory this small defeat, adding it to the others.

He'd gotten up from the table early because Marcel, his cousin, had been making faces with his mouth full of porridge, and he sensed that an all too familiar drama was brewing in the kitchen: His aunt Albertine's third warning was usually followed by a smack on the head, and after the smack came a slap, and after the slap.... On this first morning of summer he hadn't felt like listening, while his aunt screamed, his own mother protested, Marcel laughed and made uglier and uglier faces, and then spit his porridge all over the table. He thought now that if he had stayed in the house he would have missed this privileged moment that had allowed him to watch the summer sink into Fabre Street like a sword, cutting off at one stroke everything that still connected it to the never-ending spring, and he smiled.

"I'm the only one who saw summer come. Even if I wasn't ready for it." He looked all around, on the outside staircases, on the balconies of the neighbouring houses, to see if any other little boy or girl was still shivering, as he was, from what had just occurred, had been an involuntary, privileged witness to a unique and precious moment, but he was the only one, and he sighed with contentment.

The diminutive Claude Lemieux, so cute in the freshly ironed clothes he felt he had a duty to get dirty as fast as he could, emerged from his house across the street and waved.

"What're you doing there? We're supposed to hand in our books this morning before the French exam and we better not be late."

The fat woman's child closed his eyes and buried his nose between his knees.

"I'll be there right away. But don't wait for me..."

He felt the weight of his textbooks against his back, all those books he'd hated or loved during the school year, but that were *books*, his great passion, what he loved most of all in the world after his parents. More than his brothers anyway: They were too old for him and they were always putting down his precociousness, claiming it was just showing-off by a child brought up among adults. The mere thought that he had to part with his books, even the ones that had brought him grief, like his arithmetic book or the atlas in which he had trouble understanding anything at all, made him sick. He had adored anything that looked like a book since he'd started school, so much so that the household was suspicious because he was definitely too young to be going around all the time with a book under his arm like some crazy old professor.

His aunt Albertine used to say: "If you ask me, that kid'll need glasses before he's ten! It wasn't enough to have one lunatic in the house, oh no, we had to have this one too!" The lunatic was obviously Marcel, who exasperated his mother more and more with his silly behaviour, like that of a much younger child, and worried her with his budding combativeness. Her nephew's excessive serenity and her son's increasingly uncontrollable agitation were driving her crazy and she yelled at both of them with equal injustice, ignoring the warnings of her sister-in-law, the fat woman, though the latter had forbidden her to quarrel with her child. Albertine generously handed out threats and punishment, finger pointing and hair flying.

The scab was softening under his tongue and starting to taste rather pleasantly of blood. He licked at it like a cat at its bowl of milk.

The front door opened and a grinning Marcel, already a mess and as red as a tomato, came out on the balcony, bowing low like a clown at the end of his act. He'd probably introduced a pause into the meal with some dumb stunt he was especially proud of. Albertine's voice exploded like a gunshot, crossing the road and disappearing into the brick front of the Brassards' house across the street: "... can't take it any more! I've had it! How am I supposed to get through this summer? School isn't even over yet and my nerves are worn to a frazzle! If I don't kill him he'll be the death of me!" Marcel shut the door, wiped the tears that were running down his cheeks. Then he pressed his forehead against the glass, catching his breath as if he'd been running.

"It's too easy getting her mad, it's hardly even fun..."

His cousin turned his head towards him.

"How come you're puffing like that?"

"She gets pissed off fast, she runs fast and she's a pain in the ass!"

Proud of his little rhyme he broke into laughter that sounded forced to his cousin, with his back arched and head thrown back, but there had been something false, some bad faith present in everything he'd done for quite a while now, that bothered everybody. Then he went over to his cousin, stretching out his foot to nudge his schoolbag.

"Why're you all upset?"

"Me, upset?"

"Don't be two-faced! You like those damn books, don't you? You wish you could keep them.... I know you...."

Too amazed to think of anything to say, the other boy was silent. Marcel sat down beside him. His cousin thought: "Oh boy, he didn't get washed this morning. Again." He smiled anyway, a little patronizingly, and looked Marcel square in the eyes.

"I know you too.... And you didn't wash this morning...."

Marcel grabbed him by the shirt collar and brought his own face close to his cousin's. He really didn't smell very good and the other boy shuddered slightly.

"Anybody can tell I didn't wash, all it takes is a nose! But it's harder to know you don't want to hand in your books, because that's inside your head! Can you do that, can you read what's inside my head? Can you?"

Marcel's eyes had changed colour all at once, with no transition. This time his cousin was quite frankly scared. Two yellowish balls were staring at him, a little too close together because the boys' faces were nearly touching, which made Marcel look disturbingly like a panic-stricken animal. The fat woman's child could read there the madness he thought was wonderful when it was directed at someone else, but terrifying when it was directed at him.

He spoke with very calculated caution. He knew that what was most important at times like this was not to upset Marcel.

"Your eyes are yellow, Marcel.... Watch out."

"They are not!"

Impatiently, Marcel pushed the other boy away. He rummaged in the schoolbag he'd set down beside him, an old cardboard briefcase his other cousin, Richard, had used for years, took out a tiny rectangular mirror he'd stolen from his sister, Thérèse, and looked at himself very closely, moving it so he could check both eyes.

"They are not yellow! Why do you always say my eyes are yellow?"

He got up and raced down the stairs, his schoolbag in one hand, his mirror in the other. When he arrived at the bottom he turned around. The other boy felt sorry for him, in his mismatched hand-me-downs nobody else wanted: Philippe's pants, a sweater of Thérèse's, originally pink, that their mother had tried to dye blue, and shoes whose source he'd forgotten, all of questionable cleanliness because Marcel could often be found huddled in a corner, lying under beds,

surrounded by dusteroos or behind the living-room
sofa. He remembered the scarecrow in *The Wizard of
Oz* that he'd seen at the Passe-Temps with Thérèse at
Easter, and he thought: "A scarecrow. That's what he
looks like. A young scarecrow. A child scarecrow."

Marcel was smiling defiantly. "Oh boy, now he's
going to give it to me...." Marcel thought carefully
before he spoke, seemed to take the time to select
each word with care, like poisoned candies.

"You aren't the only one! I saw it come too, you
know!" The fat woman's child realized that Marcel was
talking about the second he had thought was his own
private treasure; he fidgeted on the step as if he wanted to get up and run away so he wouldn't have to
hear what his cousin had to say. Marcel was getting
worked up, talking louder and faster. "In between two
yells. I saw it arrive in between two of Mama's yells.
But *I* had time to get ready for it, not like you! Since
yesterday! I knew about it ever since yesterday! I was
warned! You know when I was wiping the tears just
now...it wasn't because Mama spanked me...it was
because I saw it come in the window when she was
spanking me. I went up to the window, I leaned on
the radiator, I stuck my nose against the screen and....
It was beautiful, wasn't it?" Marcel climbed one step,
then another. "You don't believe me — as usual! You
think you're the only one that feels things!" The fat
woman's child had frowned as he always did when
Marcel told him something extraordinary. He listened
with great concentration, hanging on his very breathing, drinking in his words, watching his mouth whenever it opened, as if to guess what was going to come
out or to feast his eyes on that strange food, those
poisoned candies he'd been dreaming about since he

was little: the ravings of Marcel, the neighbourhood laughing stock, that were fascinating to him. Marcel was almost threatening as he climbed a few more steps. "Did it say hello and bow to you? I bet it didn't. For sure it didn't! But it did to me!" Now he was kneeling on a step, still clutching his mirror and his schoolbag. "I'm the one the summer bowed to, understand? And this summer is mine too! Mine! Just because you stole the first second from me, it doesn't mean you're going to steal the rest, understand?" His cousin rose slowly, descended the few steps between them, and crouched in front of the trembling youth. "What did you see exactly? Tell me what you saw, Marcel!"

Everything disappeared from Marcel's face now — the anger, the elation, the brilliant yellow of his eyes, the crease that appeared on his forehead when he was going to say something important. The fat woman's child looked down and sighed. "His face is fading away. He won't tell me anything else now." Marcel stowed the little rectangular mirror, took his time fastening the straps of his bag, didn't budge when his cousin ran his hand through his hair. "There's some brains inside, isn't there?" Marcel didn't even lift his head. "Yeah, there is. And they're mine!"

The big boy was dawdling along a few steps behind the little one. They didn't really seem to be travelling together, but when one of them turned a corner the other turned too; when the smaller boy crouched down to tie a shoelace the other waited, looking down at the cracks in the sidewalk, or up at a tree. The bigger boy never caught up with the smaller one so they could walk side-by-side. It was an unchanging ritual whose rules, surely unplanned, had imposed themselves one by one, thin layer by thin layer, at times imperceptible, at times obvious, but both children had accepted them without asking any questions. When had it been decided, for instance, that the bigger boy would always stay a few paces behind the other? If questioned, both would have replied that it had always been that way, they'd never noticed, or if pushed they'd say it wasn't so because they remembered that once....

Marie-Sylvia, who was very old now and starting to fantasize about her childhood in the country from the back of her usually deserted store, called them the geese, even though there'd never been any geese on her father's farm. All she knew was that geese go around in a compact flock led by a head goose — probably a female, but she wasn't positive — who leads her flock simply by going to the head of the squad. She said to the ghost of Duplessis, her cat who had vanished one morning in the spring of 1942: "Look, there go the two geese.... I'll never understand why they don't walk together; they're cousins, after all! Anyhow, there's not much a person can understand in that house!"

When the smaller boy was with his gang of pals — Claude Lemieux, Carmen and Manon Brassard, the other Carmen, Madame Ouimet's, or the Jodoin children — the bigger one would disappear or, rather, he wouldn't appear at all, as if he were letting them take his place when he was sure he couldn't be alone with his cousin. But that morning they were a sorry sight, walking listlessly past Marie-Sylvia's store where she was sweeping her stretch of sidewalk and griping about her aching back. Dust swirled around her, then landed again, exactly where she had disturbed it. But she did this religiously, every morning from May to October, and she was convinced she had the cleanest doorway in the neighbourhood when what she actually had were the dustiest clothes. Spying them across the street, Marie-Sylvia stood motionless in her cloud of dust, leaning on the broom with her chin on her hands. "Would you look at the geese! You certainly don't look like two kids getting ready for summer holidays!" They turned their heads at the same moment, simultaneously raised their hands to wave, neither one smiling. Marie-Sylvia watched despondently till they'd turned the corner onto Gilford Street. "Did you ever see anything like it, Duplessis? Amazing, the way they do everything together! They're only cousins, after all, not twins! Who ever heard of twins born five years apart? And with different mothers?" Muttering, she went back to her broom while flames shot through her aching back.

Gilford Street was full of noisy schoolchildren of all ages, from little kids in Grade One who didn't know the meaning of the word "exams" and therefore didn't understand why the others were so nervous, to pimply-faced Grade Nines, the "big kids," who generally terrorized the other kids because they were older and stronger and knew more, but who on this important morning only made a racket and didn't threaten anybody with a punch on the shoulder or a smack on the head. It was noisy, yes, but less so than usual: A nearly tangible menace hovered above the restless little crowd, in a sense robbing of excitement this road to school that was so often the theatre for resolving some drama (pitched battles between gangs of boys from warring streets were not uncommon) or some blooming rivalry. The boys who lived on nearby streets — Papineau, Marquette, Fabre, Garnier — poured onto Gilford every morning, and encounters there weren't always happy ones.

As for the girls, who hadn't the slightest interest in the boys' spats, they had long ago learned to take Saint-Joseph Boulevard to the École des Saints-Anges: They would cross Gilford to the sound of nicknames, even insults, from the boys they met, then continued north as if they hadn't heard a thing. Then they'd swoop onto Saint-Joseph, shrieking and hugging and grabbing each other around the waist — except in winter, obviously, when heavy clothes meant that nobody *had* a waist — and skipped to school, telling each other anything that would bring a laugh.

Loving couples though, and starting in Grade Eight there were plenty of those, often had a serious dilemma: whether to turn bravely onto the boys' street at the risk of the girl arriving at school in tears from being ridiculed and humiliated — a girl who hangs around with guys is the next best thing to a whore — or to go up to the girls' boulevard and risk the boy arriving at his school tomato-red from being the target of so many clucking, sighing females if he was cute, or cruel, mocking ones if he had ears that stuck out like barn doors or overly aggressive acne.

And so Marcel and his cousin didn't attract the other boys' attention when they turned the corner that morning, to the relief of the fat woman's child. Claude Lemieux was waiting for him at the corner of Garnier. When he gestured helplessly, indicating his cousin behind him, Claude shrugged impatiently and ran off towards school.

And that was where the little boy realized he'd forgotten to cross Gilford Street before heading west. Now they'd have to walk past the house at 1474! Feeling lost, he stopped smack in the middle of the sidewalk. His cousin, who for once wasn't paying attention to his every move, bumped into him and seemed to emerge from his torpor only when he too realized where they were. On their left, a tiny front yard, maybe eight feet square, filled with bleeding hearts and surrounded by a low metal fence painted black, dressed up what was otherwise a perfectly ordinary house. But the sight of that innocent yard produced conflicting reactions in the two boys: Marcel smiled and immediately placed his hands on his cousin's shoulders, while the younger boy started to twist and moan as if in the throes of a nightmare. Marcel, afraid he'd run away, grabbed hold of him and nestled his chin in his cousin's neck.

"Let's take a little walk in the enchanted forest, okay?"

Marcel's voice tickled his cousin's ear uncomfortably and he raised his own voice as he struggled.

"We haven't got time, Marcel, we really haven't! I can't be late, we have exams today."

A big Grade Nine boy went past them, ruffling Marcel's hair.

"Too late for kisses, lovebirds, the bell's about to ring. Unless you take the boulevard with the sissies!"

After elbowing his way to freedom, the fat woman's child ran a few steps, but his cousin caught him right away. This time the embrace was more violent, and it took his breath away. Marcel's voice was more halting too, and he knew he was going to be late for school.

Marcel was laughing now.

"I haven't got exams and you know it, I'm in the supplementary class! I'll draw my pictures like I always do and they'll give me a good mark so they won't have me around for too long! They'll get rid of me, but not you!"

The little boy felt himself being lifted up and carried; a kick unhooked the front gate, hinges creaked, bunches of bleeding hearts whipped his face, and then he was on his back in the damp earth. He felt his schoolbooks against his shoulder blades and thought: "I have to stay on my back, I can't let him take my books away!"

He had gotten to know the enchanted forest in spite of himself. He'd realized for a long time that Marcel had a summer hiding place somewhere in the neighbourhood, under a gallery, in some backyard, or behind the stairs to a shed, where he spent hours daydreaming, but he'd never been curious enough to look for it because it was a relief just knowing such a place existed: While Marcel was dreaming in his hole he didn't have to keep an eye on him and he could join his friends with a clear conscience.

Marcel began disappearing around the middle of May, as soon as the buds had opened. He would set off on a Saturday morning with a jam sandwich and a half-pint of milk and not come back till late afternoon, transformed, calmer, and almost a pleasure to be around. His mother, who normally would have been worried about this disappearance, but was secretly glad to have a few hours of peace, would give him a token scolding, without much conviction. He said: "You knew I was going for the day, you even packed me a lunch!" She replied: "I was worried anyway! The parks aren't open yet! Where were you all day for heaven's sake, you're covered with dirt! At your age you shouldn't be playing in the dirt!" But the next day he asked for another sandwich, and she complied without asking any questions.

He often boasted to his cousin about a wonderful spot that only he knew about, an inviolable hiding place, an enchanted forest that was his alone, where anything was possible if you had a bit of imagination, a hiding place where it didn't rain when it's raining, where it wasn't too hot when it's hot because you're in the shade, a perfectly round, perfectly smooth bubble that cut him off from the rest of the world. His vocabulary was transformed when he talked about the enchanted forest: He went from the limited language he used at home and didn't always take the trouble to enunciate properly, to a kind of poetry, primitive but colourful, that his cousin with his literary sensitivity found quite appealing — and envied in him a little too.

One day, the fat woman's child had dutifully checked out all the bushes in the neighbourhood, though they were few in number and mostly puny and pitiful, but he'd found nothing because he'd concentrated on the lanes and backyards: it would never have occurred to him that such a unique spot, totally inaccessible to the rest of world and as peaceful as a grave according to Marcel, could be found right on Gilford Street, just a few feet from the cars roaring by or from a cluster of little girls playing hopscotch. In the end he actually suspected the place didn't really exist, that Marcel just roamed the neighbourhood all day, even venturing outside the limits of Plateau Mont-Royal — which, needless to say, they were both strictly forbidden to do — and that his enchanted forest was just another invention of the overactive imagination for which Albertine had chided her son over so many years. And so he let his cousin rave about his hiding place and in the end always told him: "Go to your enchanted forest, jerk, if it's all that wonderful!" End of discussion. Within five minutes Marcel would disappear with a superior little smirk, the fat woman's child would join his friends, and for a few hours he'd forget the very existence of this weird cousin he still wasn't sure if he loved or hated, but accepted something like a punishment he didn't deserve.

This went on until early September when school started again — that accursed time, still so beautiful though you think it's finished now, summer's over, but there's still a whole month of fine weather before the leaves turn red all at once and autumn comes and hits you in the face. All summer, then, Marcel made himself scarce in the daytime and left his cousin in peace. Nights, of course, were another matter. The house was big, with plenty of nooks and crannies. And Marcel could run faster than his cousin.

On the day in question that previous August, Marcel had been hovering around his cousin all afternoon. No way to get rid of him, though the little boy tried everything: insults and threats, even though Marcel was much bigger and much stronger, pleading, promises of Mell-O-Rolls or orange popsicles.... Nothing could budge Marcel, who stuck like a fly. The fat woman's child couldn't play with his friends, who wanted nothing to do with Marcel, calling him "pigeon" because the whole neighbourhood said he had the walk and the brains of a pigeon. And so the two of them had wandered along Fabre Street on their own, from staircase to staircase, from stoop to stoop, square of dirt to square of dirt, from Gilford to Mont-Royal, the little boy exasperated by his cousin's stubbornness, the other pitiful but excited by something he wanted to share but didn't dare express.

They were crouched over a dandelion that had long since gone to seed when Marcel said point-blank: "We're going to Guimond's now, I got something to show you...."

Chez Guimond was a restaurant something like Marie-Sylvia's, but further from the house — it was at the corner of Gilford and Brébeuf — and the children from Fabre Street seldom went there, partly because of the distance but mainly on account of the owner, a hunchback who scared off all the kids in the parish because he didn't want their business. He'd been saying that all children are thieves ever since the time he'd caught Marcel with his hand in the candy jar, and he invariably went berserk whenever a human being under fifteen showed up.

Marcel's proposal startled his cousin.

"Go to Guimond's? Are you crazy? You want to come home with one nut missing?"

Marcel, who had taught his cousin to use the word "nut" in this way ("testicle" wasn't yet part of his vocabulary and even if it were, he'd have thought it sounded pompous), thought this was hilarious, and he laughed so hard he fell onto his back on the Sauvés' scruffy lawn. His cousin was relieved to see him laughing; since that morning he'd been worried about one of the inexplicable fits that came over Marcel more and more often, always after a period of melancholy like the one he'd been going through in the past few hours. Albertine often said: "When Marcel sticks too close get out the wooden spoon: The fit's on its way."

Marcel wiped his eyes with the edge of his pale blue cotton sweater, another hand-me-down from Thérèse that still smelled a little bit like her.

"If Monsieur Guimond cut off my nut he'd say it was an olive and sell it!"

He turned onto his back again, pounded the earth with both feet, as he shouted happily and rolled in the grass. Relieved, his cousin looked on, thinking: "Go ahead and laugh, then you'll forget about me and I can get out of here." It went on for a while, at some moments nearly hysterical, and at others with Marcel more relaxed and less frenetic. But it was still amazing to see him convulsed with laughter over something so trivial, and after a while the fat woman's child frowned. "Seems to me he ought to be over it by now." Gradually Marcel calmed down, with an occasional jolt of laughter that seemed to leave him exhausted. Finally he turned to his cousin, still red-faced but completely recovered.

"Laughing feels good, doesn't it?"

The fat woman's child pulled a blade of grass and stuck it in his mouth.

"Yeah, but why do you only laugh at stupid things?"

He hadn't had time to react when Marcel was already on top of him. Now he was on his back, as he would be on a June morning a year from now, with Marcel's weight on him, and overhead, a square of blue sky with some drifting clouds.

"What makes *you* laugh, huh? The mean things people say about me? Is that it?"

He was immobilized, his wrists pinned to the grass, legs hobbled by Marcel's knees. He thought: "I'll be black and blue again and Mama'll think I was fighting...." He took a deep breath and tried to smile but his lips were quivering slightly. The grass had fallen out of his mouth and it was tickling his cheek in a

25

way he hated. Another few seconds and it would slide over towards his right nostril. Sheer torture. He had to think of something to say that would distract Marcel, dispel the looming anger, let him gain some time. Either that or give in. Which he did, telling himself that Monsieur Guimond probably wouldn't let them in his store anyway, especially not Marcel.

"What makes me laugh is Monsieur Guimond's hump. It's so big it's like another head!"

He had won. Marcel's attention shifted back to the subject of their original conversation and a glimmer of mirth appeared in his eyes, which had been darkened by anger. He relaxed his grip so quickly that the fat woman's child thought something was fishy, they weren't on their way to Guimond's, Monsieur Guimond and his hump were only a defeat, an excuse for Marcel, and he himself had fallen into a trap he'd seen coming but couldn't avoid. As soon as he was free he realized it would have been smarter to lie there on the ground all afternoon instead of following Marcel. But never *ever* would it cross his mind to run away from Marcel. Past attempts to do so had cost him dearly: They lived in the same house, one that was a tight squeeze for its ten inhabitants, and the nooks and crannies where a preying beast could take its victim were unfortunately all too many. He preferred to pay now, with no interest, in broad daylight.

That time, the only time, it had been the smaller boy who had followed the other. Marcel had egged him on, called him a slowpoke, run up to Gilford Street, come back, hopped up and down so excitedly his cousin had had a vision of someone sentenced to death — himself — on his way to the scaffold (medieval stake? guillotine? kettle of boiling oil?)

behind a fool in a red and green outfit covered with little bells, who was jumping around like a monkey. Caught up in his own game he hunched his shoulders, imagined himself shivering with cold and fright in a rough homespun robe that chafed his skin, dragging his feet to keep from losing the bloody bandages that were coming loose, pulling off strips of flesh that attracted flies. The sky was low over France and the crowd that reeked of sweat and onions was silently waving its fists. What had he done to deserve this promenade at dawn that was taking him towards his Creator? Had he saved a princess in a pointed head-dress? Spat on an effigy of the king? Was he an underground hero — Robin Hood, yes, yes, Robin Hood...but this wasn't France any more, and it wasn't the Middle Ages! — who had finally been captured and now was about to be torn limb from limb, decapitated, quartered, and thrown to ravenous dogs for three days and three nights? He was hypnotizing himself, diverting his attention from reality to avoid thinking about being at Marcel's mercy. Once again he chose dreaming, because what he'd have to live through in the next few minutes certainly wasn't going to be fun. He always did that when his brothers tormented him, when his aunt Albertine yelled at him, when his mother tried to reason with him. Robin Hood was always close by when there were obstacles, or Peter Pan when he felt he had to fly away to escape a brewing storm.

As he was turning onto Gilford, in fact, he felt the need to get rid of the ball-and-chain he'd been lugging around, to slip into Peter Pan's green costume and fly away, laughing: the galleries would seem to sink into the earth, he would brush against the trees, against gravel-covered roofs, and then the sky, at last the sky, no bonds now, the breast-stroke through the clouds, the crawl through the endless expanse of blue, then some dives, somersaults, spirals — and freedom.

When he let himself come to his senses again after these endless capers among birds wild with joy because he'd joined them, he was not outside Monsieur Guimond's store but at the little fence that ringed the little front yard in front of the little house at 1474 Gilford, and Marcel had just put his arms around him like a young bride at the end of an American movie. He had cried out, a single pitiful little cry, like a cat disturbed in its sleep. And then he let himself be led into the enchanted forest of his cousin Marcel, the parish lunatic. Finally, he was going to know.

It was cool, surprisingly so after the mugginess of August. You were a little dazed at first in the half-light, dazed to find yourself both in the dark and on your hands and knees. You stayed there, motionless and all ears, *listening* to this suspect place whose existence was so unexpected you'd never have guessed it was there. You told yourself, Okay, it's dark, it's cold, I'm a little bit scared, but I have to do something.... So you reached out your arm and then you realized just how small this place was. That reassured you — a little. Your heels touched the fence, your outstretched arm the brick of the house. On the left you guessed at the gallery where the neighbourhood cats came to piss in peace (you wrinkled your nose, the smell was so strong); on your right the fence again, but dirty, never painted, rusty, twisted by sudden thaws, loose from the wall. When your eyes had got used to the darkness you looked up. Bunches of bleeding hearts brushed your forehead; everything was pink and green, with little spots of blue when the wind blew and ruffled the diminutive grove. And then, you couldn't help it, you lay on your back, delighted: It was a flowery grave where you were cut off from everything and its charm was irresistible. Everything was possible here. Especially your wildest dreams.

He understood all that within a few seconds, even before he'd experienced it: He projected himself forward in time, saw himself loving this incomparable place, spending hours here or days, enraptured, oblivious to everything, absolutely everything, what was beautiful in his life and what was ugly, to devote himself entirely to the treasures of this enchanted forest.

"Shove over, my nose is in your rear end!"

The fat woman's child jumped. He'd completely forgotten that Marcel was there. His fear had evaporated. He felt good. He moved aside, groping his way, his left hand pressed against the wall of the house. The cold brick was covered with moss. So the sun never shone here. Even in winter? He tried to remember the position of the house in relation to the sun. That's right, the sun didn't shine here, not even in winter. Maybe an hour or two in the late afternoon...a feeble little sun that probably didn't even come all the way to the brick when the snow was piled up. A wall untouched by sunlight!

He stayed motionless while Marcel inched his way toward him, negligently shoving aside the bleeding hearts like someone who feels at home and doesn't have to bother being careful. Already too present in his own hiding-place. The fat woman's child understood that the enchanted forest would never belong to him. He was on a visit here, perhaps his only one: Marcel was going to show him around, singing the praises of his private kingdom and then showing him the door, cutting off his access forever.

A car drove past along Gilford, or rather the sound of a car, because you couldn't see anything through the roots, stems, branches that had long ago launched their attack on the metal fence. He looked in the direction of the sound, even turned his head towards the right when the car stopped at the corner of Fabre to park.

"In July I couldn't come here for a whole week 'cause the woman decided to paint her fence! Crazy old fool! Everything got mixed up for days: flowers were falling all over the place, she spilled black paint on the branches, and it stank to high heaven! I couldn't wait for her to be done! I was afraid she'd cut it all down... She talked to Marie-Sylvia about it... That really had me scared! But she got fed up before she'd finished so then I could come back...."

"Is she old?"

"Is who old?"

"You know, the woman...."

"You mean you never saw her? She's always sitting on her gallery."

"No, I never noticed.... I've never looked.... I never come here in the summer...."

"Make up your mind! You never come here or you never look when you do?"

Marcel was behaving like himself again. The fat woman's child didn't bother answering. And Marcel probably didn't expect him to anyway. Two little girls went past singing "Mary, Mary, dictionary, tell me the name of the one I will marry," without a skipping rope. He thought they were particularly dumb.

"Yeah, she's old. That's why it took her so long just to do part of the fence... She's bent so bad she didn't have to scrunch down to paint the bottom." He patted his thigh. His cousin shrugged. "I suppose you'll say she doesn't scrunch down to tie her shoes either...." Marcel leaned towards him. "I'm the one that makes the jokes in here! It's *my* place!" The fat woman's child leaned against the cold brick. The time had come. "So why'd you bring me here?"

It had started very gently: an inaudible murmur that rose no higher than the first branches of the bleeding hearts, a whispering so soft, so low, so barely articulated, it was more like the wail of a newborn, a confession so hard to express it didn't really assume a shape, unless it was he who didn't know how to listen. No, he was sure he knew how to listen, especially to those things that were so hard for others to let out. Yes, it was Marcel who had trouble expressing himself. It was whispered, yet it was addressed to him, and so he leaned towards his cousin, the better to hear him. He'd been a little more aware of the smell of sweat that followed Marcel everywhere, but the words — if they really were words — still escaped him. He guessed at Marcel's profile in the half-light, the fine domed forehead he envied because he'd read somewhere that it was a sign of great intelligence, maybe even genius, his feverish eyes, so intense at moments like this, the nose and mouth that jutted out in what Albertine called his "poet's pout," which she tried to correct with well-aimed clouts. He was very close to his cousin's profile, perhaps an inch or two away, and he felt an urge to reach out his lips, to place them on his temple, which he imagined damp despite the coolness. But can you kiss your twelve-year-old cousin on the temple out of the blue like that? Especially when he's hesitated for a whole day and now he's finally agreed to open up, to unburden himself to you? Would a kiss, no matter how sincere, put an end to everything? Would Marcel stop talking? And what about the enchanted forest: Would it burst like a bubble leaving him under the outside staircase on Fabre Street, drained, exhausted, broken, as he was at the end of his own flights? He felt something warm rise from his belly, lower than his belly even, then it swept into his lungs and made his heart contract. His eyes filled with tears and he said in a murmur hardly clearer than his cousin's: "Speak up, Marcel, I can't hear a thing."

The first words he caught were the names of colours: rose, violet, mauve. Thinking Marcel was talking about the bleeding hearts, he raised his head. A flower tickled his nose. With the back of his hand he brushed it aside the way you get rid of a bee. It landed on Marcel's thigh but he didn't notice. Next came the name of a city: Florence. Florence was in Italy, he'd learned that recently because when Frère Robert came back from Italy where he'd seen Pope Pius XII in the flesh he told them the whole city of Florence was a museum and all thirty Grade Four pupils came out with a unanimous "Yuck!" that their teacher found very depressing. Could Marcel be talking about the colours in Florence? But why? Then all at once came the name of a politician the entire family hated: Duplessis. What did Duplessis have to do with Florence? He'd have to look in *La Presse* and see if the Premier of Quebec was on a trip to Italy.... Why all this fuss and mystery just to say that Duplessis was in Florence? He was about to leave here, abandon Marcel

and the enchanted forest, laugh at his cousin's pretensions — after all, this place was nothing but a yard
nobody looked after and it wasn't the slightest bit
enchanted — when Marcel abruptly turned his head
so that their noses nearly touched. He thought to himself that he'd never been so close to someone else's
face except maybe his mother's when she flung herself
at him and nibbled his cheeks, saying they were as
red as fall apples. He'd never seen a face so overcome
by emotion, so pleading; he didn't even know such a
face could exist. He pulled back, the brick cut into his
cotton shirt, and he felt little prickles of warmth
between his shoulder-blades. *I'm going to bleed....*
Marcel had lowered his head. No more words came
from his mouth. No colours, no city, no Premier of
Quebec. *I'd better ask him something. He* has *to talk! I*
have *to understand what he's talking about!*

But Marcel had already raised his head. And then
everything came out at once: all his insanity, or what
his family saw as insanity, all his dreams that maybe
weren't dreams after all, everything that had happened
to him over the past ten years since he was a small
child: the ecstasies and the despondency; the moments
of certainty and the gnawing doubts; the fervor and
the sluggishness; the presents, the gifts, the consola-
tions of Rose, Violette, and Mauve, and their mother,
Florence — now his cousin realized they weren't
colours or a city but...but what? — the energy he had
inside him that came out all twisted because he didn't
have the head, he didn't have the wits, because he
couldn't find a way to use it; everything: his piano
lessons, his golden voice, his poems, all those things
that made him so happy as long as he was in the
house of Rose, Violette, and Mauve, who disappeared
as if they'd never existed as soon as he was gone (he

described in detail his visit to the music store five years earlier and how his mother had humiliated him, but his cousin couldn't understand a thing), every-thing, yes, everything, especially the cat Duplessis, the great love between them, their complicity, their defini-tive alliance that ordinarily nothing should have disturbed because you don't interfere with perfection. It went on for a long time, suddenly it was being very clearly enunciated, almost recited, like poetry, it sent him into a rapture that gave the existence of the enchanted forest its full meaning: The fat woman's child understood vaguely that this cave of bleeding hearts was the only place outside Florence's house where Marcel's genius could be expressed. He was overcome with happiness at his cousin's images sent through the ceiling of flowers, birch bark canoes that sailed through the summer sky, steered by the devil himself or by someone who strangely resembled him, by mad choruses of old old songs, by tapping feet that broke your heart while you were dazzled by the violins, complete symphonies executed in just one second that exploded in a single universal note, by colour harmonies laid down like sacred offerings, by scraps of poems so beautiful they changed you for-ever, by things of devastating beauty. Now Marcel's face was close to his, his eyes trying to read in his own. The question was peremptory, vital, absolute: "Do you understand? *Do you understand?*"

"No. But go on."

And he did. *Don't let it come to an end, ever! Don't let him run out of the words that will let him go on, let him make this...this happiness last forever.*

The spring dried up as quickly as it had appeared. Marcel stopped almost in mid-sentence. At any rate his cousin couldn't grasp the last words. Both were left dangling, each one wanting to hold out his arms to the other and ask for help. And that was all. It smelled of cat pee again and the fence on their right was rust-eaten once more.

At this one moment of mutual communion they experienced the desperate intensity of a dream that has shattered into irretrievable pieces. Here, in this enchanted forest, their paths had touched and now they would branch off again and separate forever.

They *saw* themselves moving apart in space and time, and simultaneously brought their hands to their mouths, to stifle a cry of despair.

The fat woman's child let a long moment pass before he asked his question, because he knew the reply would be essential but that he wouldn't understand it.

"Why'd you tell me that today?"

Marcel's cry was so desperate that the fat woman's child told himself he would never, ever set foot in this place again, never ever approach the eternal, the absolute that he sensed in his cousin's confession.

"Because there's starting to be holes in Duplessis!"

For close to a year the fat woman's child had avoided walking past the enchanted forest. Whether surrounded by his friends or with Marcel in tow he never turned immediately left at the corner of Gilford and Fabre; he would cross Gilford, then carefully look straight ahead so the house at 1474 wouldn't enter his field of vision. Marcel realized what he was doing and his cousin often heard snickering over his shoulder, a tiny snicker, barely audible, but that jostled him as if Marcel had shoved him from behind. Every time, he was bowled over by the vicious laughter and he'd think: "I won't come this way any more, I'll take the girls' road to school...." But his pals would never have forgiven him and even the girls, though they adored him, wouldn't have looked on kindly if this kid, who didn't have a girlfriend and therefore had no reason to be there, were to join their group with their giggling and their secrets on his way to school. It would make him an anomaly for the others to point at. When he was with the Jodoin brothers and Claude Lemieux he managed to get sufficiently carried away to forget — almost — about the existence of the enchanted forest across the street, but whenever Marcel dogged his footsteps he would feel the moment coming when those quick little mocking notes would be stuck in his back like so many poisoned darts.

They had never talked again about Rose, Violette, and Mauve, about Duplessis or the *chasse-galerie*, that magical canoe. Marcel had uttered a solitary cry of distress to which there was to be no reply because that was how he wanted it. His cousin could read in his eyes that the secret was sealed, that Marcel regretted the momentary weakness that had made him open up to his cousin; he quickly realized that this communion, which had lasted a few hours, had not brought them together but driven them apart, permanently: Marcel had cried out for help, then he'd covered the mouth of the person he had called upon because he didn't *want* to be saved. Or knew that he couldn't be. He had exposed one small corner of the turmoil that filled him, then changed his mind completely about sharing it. But instead of carrying on as if that August afternoon had never existed, instead of deliberately choosing oblivion and total silence, he never missed a chance to remind his cousin, snickering, that something significant had almost passed between them, until he himself had decided to nip it in the bud. They never talked about it, but it was always there; it had lasted for just a few seconds, and even then it didn't happen every day, but when the thing, the silent recollection, the inexpressible secret showed itself so cruelly, in the middle of a snowstorm for instance, when the wind made walking difficult, or on a radiant day when the white of the snow and the blue of the sky exploded with joy, the fat woman's child wanted to die. From humiliation, from shame, and from envy. Especially envy.

Marcel, though, wasn't altogether convinced that his snicker was only meant for his cousin. He often felt as if he were laughing at himself. Because he'd never gone back to the enchanted forest either, and the mere sight of 1474 Gilford still rankled. He had spent that summer prowling around but never going inside; he'd seen the leaves turn red, turn yellow, and fall, he'd seen the bed they formed as they dried, seen the old woman raking them into a pile by the side of the street that slow-moving jokers would burn. Then the snow fell and covered the enchantment for six long months. But even in the spring, even during the blessed season of lilac and lily-of-the-valley when Montreal smelled like First Communion, Marcel hadn't dared to violate his old sanctuary. He often came and stood in front of the iron fence, but he never went inside. After having been the absolute master of that place, he had become the sentinel who guards the entrance, and it was killing him.

But today it was summer, and to come full circle, or perhaps so he wouldn't have to listen to his own snickering any more, Marcel had kidnapped his cousin and had unhesitatingly crossed the threshold of his own imagination.

"Get off, Marcel, you weigh a ton...."

Marcel didn't move. On the contrary he pressed on his belly as hard as he could to swell it up and smother his cousin a little more.

"You don't make the laws around here...."

"I didn't ask to come, you dragged me here! I just want to go to school and write my exam...."

Marcel seemed to find this funny. His smile creased his cheeks and forehead, and the fat woman's child thought: "Sometimes my thirteen-year-old cousin acts like he's eighty...." Marcel shook his head the way the fat woman did when she was at once discouraged and glad; he brought his tongue against the roof of his mouth to produce an unpleasant "tsk, tsk" exactly the way she did, and his cousin thought: "My thirteen-year-old cousin can even look like my mother when he wants...." The little yellow light glimmered in Marcel's eyes even before his expression changed; for a few seconds he was at once an amused old man, the discouraged fat woman, and Marcel on the verge of a fit, and the other boy thought: "But now my thirteen-year-old cousin's crazy again."

He didn't want to suffer one of Marcel's fits in this precarious position. Once again, he'd have to try to make his cousin think about something else. He took a deep breath, felt the corners of his books against his shoulder-blades and the tears that stung his eyes and, thinking of a bridge, of a little boy straddling the parapet of the bridge and watching the cold water come closer and closer before it swallowed him, he asked: "Are there still holes in Duplessis?" This question had been running through his mind since the previous August. He had turned it in every direction — he knew Duplessis was an imaginary cat who talked and had taught Marcel a good part of what he knew, that a great friendship had united them for ten years now, but what did holes have to do with it? He'd spent long hours at night trying to penetrate the mystery and often he came to the brink of what he thought was the solution, but then he would waken with a start and think: "I was asleep! I figured it out in my sleep but now I can't remember!" Sometimes he would envision Duplessis like a big piece of cheese, sometimes like the spaghetti strainer his mother had got for Christmas. He saw Marcel pick up Duplessis and stick his fingers through him, but that was so disgusting he had to chase the image from his mind before he was sick to his stomach.

The slap that landed on his face now brought him fully back to himself: There was no bridge now, no parapet, no water, no cheese or spaghetti strainer, just Marcel's face which was grimacing in a disturbing way. His cheeks were red and burning, hands clutched at his shoulders, he felt himself being lifted and then flung backwards, the corners of his books cut off his breathing, and he heard his aunt Albertine whispering on the balcony of the house on Fabre Street a few nights earlier, when she and the fat woman were drinking a Coke without suspecting he was listening — though he was an inveterate eaves-dropper: "I'm afraid he'll turn violent. I can see it coming in his eyes. And I know he could destroy us all."

Marcel had brought his mouth close to his own, his breath smelled terrible but the fat woman's child put up with it because he thought his cousin was on the verge of a major revelation. But Marcel wasn't able to speak now exactly as he had done the year before: Words that didn't come out, inarticulate sounds like the squalls of a dreaming baby emerged from his lips, his eyes that had been angry a few seconds earlier now were pleading as if he was urging his cousin to speak for him, to find the right words and enunciate them, to put them in the proper order and to form, once and for all, the liberating phrase they'd both been waiting for, and for such a long time. And that was exactly what happened. Without even understanding what he was saying, in particular without knowing the source of the sentence that was emerging from his wicked mouth, the fat woman's child's said to himself in Marcel's voice, a counterfeit Marcel's voice: "The holes ate up Duplessis, now all I see is his eyes!"

He felt Marcel's relief as if it were his own, and for a fraction of a second he saw Duplessis, saw three images of Duplessis though the cat had been dead for ten years now: first a magnificent tiger-striped tomcat smiling, yes, smiling at him, an adorable, absolutely irresistible animal you felt you could trust with your life because you knew *he* would do something with it; then that strange thing, a cat, the same cat, but now you could see right through him because holes, real holes, had appeared in him as if something were eating him from inside, something that resembled deception because somebody — who could be no one but yourself — had betrayed him; and finally, two eyes with a few hairs around them, a muzzle moist at the tip, and above it all, two pointed ears. And that was all. Everything else had been eaten away. Again by deception, by betrayal. A tongue passed over the muzzle and you felt like doing the same. But the smile had vanished too and your heart melted because something that resembled a broken voice was telling you: "You let me down. You let me down so badly."

The image drifted away and the fat woman's child realized he was holding onto his cousin with all the strength in a nine-year-old's arms. Water was running down his neck. Snot too. And a jerky, broken sob rose up amid the bleeding hearts: "I miss him so much! You can't imagine how I miss him! He was my whole life! He was the only one that mattered!" And he realized that he too was missing something, was missing a cat he'd never known but that was absolutely essential to his own survival. He rested his head against his cousin's, stuck his ear against the other boy's, perhaps in the hope of hearing the wonders that were hidden there.

School, handing in his textbooks, exams — nothing existed now but a tremendous unhappiness that was being lived by a little boy who was weak in the head.

He stood on his tiptoes and looked inside the classroom. The usual relative calm had been replaced by the coming and going of happy boys who were here to throw at their teachers' feet the source of their headaches, the object of their resentment, the cause of a good part of their punishments: their textbooks. Frère Robert stood in the midst of a pile of books bound in red, green, or grey from which they had just torn the brown paper covers that lay around the desks now every which way.

As soon as their names were called they stepped over the greasy, torn, ink-spotted papers, ran up to the teacher, rid themselves once and for all of the math book, the Grade Four atlas, the catechism, or the detested French grammar book, then returned to their seats unburdened, relieved, and smiling. You could recognize individual personalities from the way they got rid of their books. Yves Trottier, the class dunce who was also the biggest blabbermouth and was said to be as nervy as the Grade Nines, sported a condescending little grin as he threw atlas and grammar against the wall to make sure they'd be unusable by next year's Grade Fours; Michel Daniel, the puniest of the thirty pupils about whom no one knew whether Michel or Daniel was his first name, set each book down after carefully wiping it on his white shirt, now white only on the sleeves and back; Claude Lemieux, the best-looking boy in school whom the others resented for being so handsome, stood in profile to the class before he bent down, for fear of being kicked in the rear; Robert "Fatso" Quevillon, a gentle, obese boy some of whose textbooks bore toothmarks (yes, yes), who either couldn't bend down or was too lazy to, stretched his arms, opened his hands, and listened delightedly as the books landed on the floor.

The ceremony, one of the most popular ones in the school year, was nearly over and the fat woman's child was glad: He hated returning his textbooks and always dreamed of keeping them even though it was forbidden. Not to mention impossible.

He would never have looked at them during the summer if he'd kept them, no, holidays are holidays, but just knowing they were there within reach if he *did* need them, filled with everything he'd learned that year and what he would try to learn next year, would have been comforting. He liked school but never bragged about it, needless to say, and the thought that somewhere, under his bed or on the bottom shelf of his brothers' bookcase where he kept books of his own, was a piece of school waiting for September, would have soothed him during the early hours of those summer nights when he felt so small, so insignificant.

He pulled open the classroom door as quietly as he could but Frère Robert saw him and stopped in the midst of calling on François Wilhelmy, the dumbest dumbbell in the class, so that it came out: "François Willl...." All heads turned towards him. He was standing in the doorway, his hair dishevelled, shirt half out of his short pants, arms covered with dirt. He was expecting the laughter that rose from the class, but not the reaction of the teacher who said only: "You look like your cousin this morning.... Take your seat, you can go after the others," then went back to calling out names. The boy walked to his desk, put down his schoolbag, opened it, and methodically emptied it while the other pupils continued trekking up and down the aisles.

After he'd piled his books on his desk he sat down and started peeling off the brown paper covers his father had helped him to cut, fold and paste last September. The stain of South Sea Blue ink at the bottom of his History of Canada brought tears to his eyes. He'd been furious about that stain when he'd made it a few weeks before, but now being separated from it broke his heart: *You aren't going to bawl your eyes out over an ink stain!* He crumpled the paper, threw it as far as he could, and realized it wasn't the ink stain that was putting him into this state. He saw again his cousin's profile, the calamity that had been hovering over the enchanted forest during Marcel's confession, and told himself that his own life had just been cut in two, that for some minutes now he was someone he didn't want to be because he wasn't ready. He hadn't been prepared for the calamity, the real one, and Marcel's despair had shaken him badly. Until then he had vaguely believed that such things only existed in books, or in the daily serials his mother and his aunt listened to on the radio from ten in the morning till two in the afternoon; but here was somebody very close to him, somebody who fascinated him but whom he'd always had a tendency to judge from on high, someone who had brought him face to face with tragedy that was incomprehensible, enormous, and from which he suspected there was no way out.

He felt a hand on his left shoulder. Claude Lemieux always smelled of bananas in the morning. Summer and winter, his mother fed him bananas and milk for breakfast and it stayed on his breath till lunch hour, earning him the nickname "Banana Split" by which he was known to the entire school. He told anyone who'd listen: "I'd rather smell of bananas than bad breath like you!" bringing any discussion to an end because the little boys at the École Saint-Stanislas were not in fact very assiduous with their toothbrushes in the morning.

"Boy, are you ever late! A whole half-hour! And there's dirt all over your back! You look like somebody dragged you to school by the feet!"

Frère Robert's voice rose a little higher.

"Lemieux, don't be such a busybody and sit down! I don't remember saying it was chitchat time...."

More laughter.

Claude Lemieux went back to his seat under the jeers of his classmates, especially Robert Quevillon who thought he looked like a girl and never missed a chance to remind him.

"You're so pretty today, Banana Split! Come here and I'll split your banana.... What do you need it for anyway?"

The fat woman's child had stripped off the last of the covers and now he was gazing at the books piled in front of him. His name hadn't been called yet. He waited. He would set them down gently, like precious objects, bid them a final farewell, even the atlas, and reluctantly leave them behind.... Suddenly realizing that the classroom had been silent for a few seconds, he looked up. Frère Robert was standing beside his desk, hands on his hips.

"Now that everybody's finished maybe you'll do us the honour of handing in your textbooks.... I hope they're cleaner than your shirt and pants...."

The child turned his head abruptly towards the window. *Ah! Peter Pan! Come and rescue me! Help me!* He pictured himself flying away with his textbooks, not dropping a single one, and hiding them...hiding them...in the enchanted forest where he knew no one would ever think of looking. He almost did it. He felt an impulse, a movement really, towards the window that was wide open to the trees on Saint-Joseph Boulevard. He felt himself sway, his heart stopped beating for a few seconds because he was giddy as he found himself suddenly in space.... The sky is deep...the books are heavy.... And what if he were to send those books raining down on Saint-Joseph Boulevard! The brother seemed to have the same idea because he put one hand on the boy's shoulder as if to keep him from flying away and letting atlases, dictionaries and grammar books land on the heads of passersby and knock them out.

"I didn't say to pitch them out the window, just bring them up to the front...."

In the ensuing scene he was more spectator than performer: he saw himself slowly get up, exactly as if he were someone else, pick up all his books, head for the podium that was surrounded by all the knowledge in the world, and open his arms to divest himself of it in one go. He saw himself standing there motionless amid the books and thinking about Marcel, who was probably already drawing a cat instead of bidding his books farewell as he'd planned to do. He thought to himself, *Look, instead of being miserable because I'm separated from my books, I'm sad because my cousin is drawing a cat full of holes.* The brother was behind him now, very close, too close. There was a smell of brother and he flinched in disgust.

"Your back is covered with dirt! Were you lying on the ground when you were supposed to be coming to school? That's a very peculiar thing to do! Another lunatic's stunt!"

The fat woman's child did what Marcel would have done. He didn't bother to turn around when he answered.

"I nearly fell asleep, it was so much nicer than it is in here!"

He was expecting a clip behind the ear; it was inevitable. His ear turned red with expectation, exactly as if the blow had been dealt.

"It's a good thing you're at the top of your class, otherwise you'd be in the Vice Principal's office, and no exam after recess!"

Good God, exams!

He had never signed his name to one of his drawings. Invariably a cat, always the same one, appeared at the bottom of every drawing he handed in to his teacher: a tiger cat, drawn sometimes in colour, sometimes in black depending on Marcel's mood, standing or lying, back arched, or sitting with his tail wrapped around his back paws, but recognizable from the sort of smile that lit up his expression, a slight modification in the way the muzzle was sketched, giving the impression the cat really was smiling. Looking at you too. Intensely. As if to ask what you thought of the drawing though he himself couldn't care less.

Frère Martial, who had been in charge of the supplementary class forever according to his colleagues (in fact he'd been the inspired instigator of them in the early forties) had followed its development with fascination. In the beginning it was square and stunted, with spindly legs and a strangely absent tail to which Marcel often gave more importance than to the drawing itself, as if it was the real subject to which the viewer's attention should be drawn. All during his first year in the supplementary class — actually it was his fifth, because they had just realized he would never learn like the other pupils — he had relegated the subject imposed by the teacher to the upper right-hand corner of the paper, to give more weight to the big cat that he drew so badly but that already had such a nice smile.

When asked about the significance of the cat, Marcel invariably replied in a peremptory tone: "It's Duplessis. He's my friend." And that was all Frère Martial could get out of him. Over the months and years, the cat had taken on its real role as a signature and Frère Martial stopped talking about it, though he kept a close eye on its development. In time the cat shrank on the page to make room for trees, houses, and other animals, but rarely for humans, and the forms became more precise, more realistic, too. And when his signature had been smallest, at the end of the previous school year, it had resembled a sketch for an attractive naïve postage stamp that Frère Martial had actually submitted to a provincial contest, but it was turned down for being too small.

The teacher had asked his pupil: "Why don't you make me a nice big drawing of Duplessis, a beautiful drawing that covers the whole page?"

And Marcel had replied: "If somebody asked you to sign your name so it covered a whole page, would you do it?"

But now, during the school year that was ending this week, Marcel's cat had been oddly transformed, becoming bigger in relation to the rest of the drawing: The sketch was childish again and what Frère Martial had taken to be spots had appeared all over the animal's body. The stripes had almost vanished, replaced by irregular circles that gave Duplessis a surprisingly savage look. The teacher started to ask Marcel if he'd seen a photo of a panther in *La Presse* or *La Patrie*, but Marcel said something that made him realize they were not spots, they were holes. Intrigued, he tried to make Marcel talk, as discreetly as possible of course so as not to frighten him, but the boy always hid behind a wisecrack: "Can't I put holes where I want?" Or a sulky silence.

During the months of May and June, though, Duplessis had almost disappeared. And just the day before, Frère Martial had seen at the bottom of Marcel's drawing a muzzle, two eyes, two pointed ears, and some whiskers.

Marcel was the first one to hand in his drawing, exactly five minutes before the start of recess, even though he'd arrived a good half-hour late and started working long after everyone else. But he'd drawn quickly, almost feverishly, with abrupt strokes that had amazed Frère Martial; he had even heaved some sighs while straightening up at his desk, as if to punctuate his unhappiness, or his frustration at being unable to render his subject the way he wanted. He seemed to want to rid himself, to free himself of something he couldn't express in a picture. His subject was resisting him and his fury was obvious.

He quietly returned to his seat after he'd dropped his drawing on the teacher's desk, and stared up at the clock, sitting motionless, hands flat on his desk. Frère Martial knew he wouldn't take his eyes off it until the bell had rung for recess.

It was a good drawing. And surprisingly, a very gentle one, that filled the whole page. Frère Martial had expected something violent, tormented, but here, at first glance anyway, was something that radiated not the anger he suspected his pupil had felt while executing it, but an apparent placidity that puzzled him. It depicted a front yard seen face on and from very low, as if the viewer's eyes were level with the bottom step. An old metal fence was doing battle with too many bleeding hearts that seemed to be choking it. On the right, you could sense the beginning of a gallery, while above it was the bottom of a window. Everything was in place, the proportions right and the colours beautiful, but a strange sensation emanated from the drawing, as if the real subject had been deliberately avoided. The fence and the bleeding hearts were concealing the real subject, which would be found somewhere in the middle of this lovely garden. Underneath the drawing. Which was not a drawing, but a screen.

Frère Martial looked at Marcel. The boy was still lost in his contemplation of the clock. He'd forgotten everything, the drawing he'd just made and where he was at this moment. Only the bell could shake him from his torpor. Was he counting the minutes, the seconds, before recess like so many of his classmates, thinking time would pass more quickly? No, he actually seemed to have taken refuge inside the clock, to have become, himself, the passing of time.

The teacher made an involuntary move that he knew was strange but he couldn't stop himself: He lifted the sheet of paper and, holding it up to the window, tried to look through it. Had Marcel made an initial drawing, then hidden it with this depiction of a garden that was so unlike him? A little laugh startled him. Marcel hadn't budged. But Monique Gratton, the only pupil in the supplementary class older than him, was giving the teacher a look of unconcealed joy. In fact she was quite bluntly laughing at him and he realized how ridiculous he must have looked. He put the drawing back on his desk. And noticed that it wasn't signed. This was the first time since he'd known Marcel. No sign of a cat, not even the moth-eaten one that had assumed such importance in his drawings over the past few months, not even the details of a head he'd seen the day before. The cat had totally disappeared and the drawing now assumed the predominant place, covering the page for the first time.

When the recess bell rang throughout the school the pupils in the supplementary class rushed at the teacher's desk without waiting for the signal, and Frère Martial found himself with a pile of drawings, half-finished or in some cases barely begun, every one more uninteresting than the rest because for most of his charges, drawing was a daily chore they'd learned to dispose of as fast as they could; he even received a blank page on which the pupil, the same one, Monique Gratton, who was hopeless at drawing and proud of it, had had the temerity to write in tiny letters: "If you want to see my pikshur look thruhg the paje." Three mistakes in eleven words — not bad for her.

Curiously, Marcel hadn't budged. He was no longer looking at the clock but sat there twiddling his thumbs, making himself as small as he could behind his desk at the back of the room, probably hoping to be forgotten. But why? Usually he was the first one out the door, yelling: "I get to have the first piss!"

Frère Martial picked up Marcel's drawing and walked over to him, coughing into his fist. Marcel looked at him blankly, as if his brain wasn't really registering the fact that someone was approaching him. The teacher put the drawing on his desk. Marcel didn't stir, except for his eyes which returned to the clock.

There was a long silence. Through the four open windows you could hear the nervous howls of the entire Saint-Stanislas elementary school, anxious about the first exam that was coming right after recess. The warning blasts of the Vice Principal's whistle were numerous because the Grade Nines took longer to settle down than the younger boys; the stampede towards the game of flag was faster, the exchange of insults between enemy camps more strident, and the victory cries when someone scored a point rose in the schoolyard with near-hysterical intensity. Four hundred children were working off their frustration before moving on to a fearsome test of memory and knowledge.

Marcel was the one who broke the silence. It was just a light-hearted observation but Frère Martial sensed a tremendous grief in his simple words, something very close to despair that had been held in for too long: "Us kids in supplementary class don't have to worry, do we? No need to get nervous, we don't write exams.... What'll we do after recess? Another drawing? How about next year when I'm in Grade Nine, do I just do more drawings? When I get out of here what else will I know how to do?"

He turned his head towards the teacher who had bent down to hear what he was saying.

The smell of sweat coming from him was characteristic, the colour of his eyes too, and the saliva dribbling onto Marcel's chin. Frère Martial started, then straightened up. He had several pupils with this disease but he hadn't known Marcel was afflicted with it too. The boy's eyes rolled back, his body tensed and began to tremble. Frère Martial took a pencil from the desk and inserted it between his pupil's teeth.

"Bite into the pencil, Marcel, let yourself go, I'll hold you...."

The seizure was brief but violent. Frère Martial took Marcel in his arms and held him tightly. The convulsive movements of the boy's thin body, his jerky gasping, the stiffness of his muscles at the peak of the seizure upset the teacher so much he started sobbing into his pupil's neck. Then he realized it was keeping Marcel from breathing normally and he laid him down on the floor of the classroom. Marcel's heels made a little sucking sound as they hit the floor. How pale he was. And thin. A scrawny little thing who would be so easy to suffocate.... The pencil had broken in half in the boy's mouth. The seizure was almost over. The teacher pulled out the two pieces of pencil. Relaxed now, Marcel seemed to sink into a deep sleep, one that only lasted a few minutes, just long enough for Frère Martial to go to the window and breathe some fresh air, to hear the bell marking the end of recess, to watch the pupils fall into line more or less silently. When he turned around, Marcel was sitting on the floor, his back against one corner of the room, and he was wiping his mouth, grimacing and moaning like a small child who has just vomited.

"You can go home now, Marcel. Come back to school on Monday...if you're feeling better."

"Don't worry about me, I'll be okay after lunch. It never lasts very long. When it's over it's over; like nothing ever happened.... I'm just a little tired."

The teacher sat on one of the desks by the window.

"Did you feel it coming for a long time?"

"What?"

"The fit...."

"No. It's all of a sudden. There's a smell...it smells like caramel, like burnt caramel, and then it's like I'm falling into space. I can't really feel what's going on. It's as if I was dizzy, that's all.... It doesn't hurt or anything. My mother says I go into confusions. Is that what you call it?"

"No. There's a scientific word for it."

"There is? What's that?"

"Epilepsy."

"Oh, yeah, I've heard that word. But my mother says it sounds too much like Pepsi. Actually, she's right about that.... I don't feel anything like a bottle of Pepsi...I feel more like...."

His gaze travelled around the classroom, lingered on the blackboard as if he was looking for a word there that would describe how he felt.

"I feel...empty. That's it...not tired, empty...."

"Does this happen very often?"

"No. Just sometimes. Funny, eh, but it's almost like it gives me a rest. Afterwards I feel empty, and rested."

"From what?"

Marcel looked him square in the eyes. His own were still slightly yellow, the pupils dilated.

"From everything. It gives me a rest from everything."

They could hear footsteps as the pupils climbed the stairs. In a few moments the classroom would be taken over by twenty turbulent youngsters who hadn't had enough time to expend all their energy and now would have a lot of trouble concentrating on anything. They would act up, they'd probably be punished, then go home furious and cursing the teacher's injustice.

Marcel picked up his drawing between thumb and forefinger and held it out to Frère Martial.

"I know what you were going to ask me. The reason Duplessis didn't sign the drawing is because this time he really drew it. And I'm not ready yet to sign it for him...."

Sure of his effect, and proud, he walked out of the classroom with hesitant little steps.

58

He spent recess looking for his cousin. They almost never talked to each other during those ten minutes of relaxation in the middle of every morning and every afternoon: Marcel stayed with the rest of his supplementary classmates who were less turbulent than the other pupils, content to walk around quietly chatting while the fat woman's child played flag or kick ball in good weather, hockey when the ice was frozen hard, or throne if there had been a snowstorm. But he liked to keep an eye on Marcel. Between two kicks of the ball or two falls on the sheer ice, he would look all around the schoolyard, register Marcel's presence in an out-of-the-way corner, roaring with laughter at Monique Gratton's antics or whispering with another classmate, often Pierre Lelièvre who lived up to his name so well (his pointed teeth were already broken), and whom everyone at school called "rabbit."

No one had ever asked the fat woman's child to keep an eye on his cousin; he did it instinctively, out of pure magnanimity, aware of a responsibility he didn't explain to himself but faced up to even when Marcel had been a real pain in the neck and he'd have been happier tearing him to shreds than protecting him: What went on outside school was their business, but at school itself so many dangers lay in wait for

Marcel and his classmates, he couldn't ignore them just because his cousin was bugging him.

The supplementary class pupils at Saint-Stanislas were very unpopular and often needed protection. You could hear them screaming with terror when the big Grade Nine boys hunted them down in their corner, calling them retards, jerks, dumbbells, or bird-brains while they dealt out clips on the head, kicks in the rear, and well-placed pinches that left arms black and blue for days. At such times he had to throw himself into the fray, often receiving blows intended for them, shouting threats everybody knew couldn't be carried out, until Frère Martial came and brought an end to the scuffle with a violence he had trouble containing. His trembling pupils, even the older ones like Marcel, would huddle around him while the Grade Nine boys ran away, clucking and cheeping like hens and chicks. The mother hen had got back her young and everything was normal again. For a while.

And then, it never failed, someone would call Marcel "pigeon," the whole schoolyard would burst out laughing, and Marcel would race inside. Usually they'd find him in one of the marble toilet stalls flushing repeatedly so he couldn't hear what was going on outside. You had to plead with him to open the door, either that or go underneath and risk getting kicked.

That morning, though, the fat woman's child didn't see his cousin's nodding head in the placid group of the supplementary class. At first he thought Marcel was in the toilet and forgot about him during the finals of a game of kick ball that his team lost pitifully. And when he noticed Frère Martial at the window a few minutes later, leaning on one hand and wiping his face with the other, it occurred to him that perhaps a pupil had felt sick and stayed inside, and that the pupil in question was Marcel. He was a little afraid of Frère Martial who had a reputation for being mean to everyone but his own pupils, so he hesitated to ask what was going on. He wanted to wave his arms to get the man's attention, but then what? Was he going to yell, "Is my cousin sick?" at the top of his lungs and risk hearing: "You mean you hadn't noticed?" from the rest of the school. But his concern won out and he was on his way to the ground-floor window when Claude Lemieux grabbed him affectionately by the neck.

"I'm so scared!"

The fat woman's child started, then pushed his friend away.

"Scared of what?"

"You know, the exams! Aren't you? Yikes — three today and four on Monday!"

The fat woman's child was already moving away.

"I haven't got time for that...."

Claude Lemieux started to skip behind his friend, the way he did when he was so nervous he couldn't contain himself. A real jack-in-the-box.

"Everybody knows you always come first, you never have problems! You just read the questions once, you answer in two seconds flat, you hand in your perfect paper, then you go home and eat your lunch like any ordinary day!"

He was holding his friend by the hand, pulling him closer as if he wanted to take him in his arms.

"I hate French so much, I can't understand a thing! They're going to ask about verbs and subjects and objects and I still don't know what they are!"

"Don't expect me to show you. Not right before

the exam! You jerk, you should've thought about that ages ago, instead of fooling around during French class!"

"I don't fool around during French and you know it. I always pay attention! And I don't understand because there's nothing *to* understand! Have you got any idea what a subordinate proposition is?"

The fat woman's child shook off his friend's embrace just as the bell rang to signal the end of recess. He looked up towards the supplementary classroom window. Frère Martial hadn't moved, but he couldn't go to see him now without getting caught. He tried to calm his apprehensions, telling himself that if Marcel was really sick Frère Martial wouldn't be at the window, he'd be taking care of him. Still, the teacher's uneasy expression gave him a pang. And he understood what it was. Marcel was having a seizure. It hadn't happened at school before. Now everybody would know and the "pigeon" would be even more of a laughing stock. Unless he begged Frère Martial not to say anything if the seizure had ended before Marcel's classmates came back.... He'd have to find a way to talk to him...a way to protect the family's well-kept secret....

He took his place in line with the others, in relative silence because the students' nerves before their first exam usually took the form of whispers they didn't even try to hide. He too could have been taken for a student terrified at the prospect of failing: his folded arms were pressed against his belly and he was bent forward slightly. But he was afraid of something very different. A long-kept secret in a household where no one dared to mention it even inside the family was liable to burst into the daylight, and shame, the shame of having somebody under your roof struck by that disease, the shame of having to admit it, to talk about it, to suffer the consequences because the others certainly wouldn't miss a chance to associate him with such a taint — the cousin of the lunatic who goes as stiff as a board and foams at the mouth — a shame that was ugly and violent had already started to twist his insides and he wished he was somewhere far away, safe in bed, in his teddy bear's arms, forever.

Claude Lemieux was standing behind him, pressing his forehead against his friend's back.

"I'm so scared I think I'll pass out...."

The mind of the fat woman's child was far from French exams or subject, verb, and object. He turned abruptly towards Claude Lemieux and shouted a little too sharply:

"You'll do the same thing you always do, you'll copy!"

Claude was so insulted he went white, as if all the blood had been taken from his body by a giant syringe.

"Copy! On an exam! Are you crazy? If I got caught I'd fail my year. My mother'd kill me! I'd have to spend the whole summer with my nose in my schoolbooks! We wouldn't be in the same class next year!"

"I can think of worse things...."

The classes got moving one after another, submissively, first Grade Nine, then Grade Eight and so on down to Grade Four, the youngest and the most undisciplined. On a nice day like today that meant two or three extra minutes of recess, which was appreciable even if they were going to pass in silence; in the winter it was less fun: There was time enough for cheeks and toes to freeze a little more and the children would stamp their feet impatiently. That day though, something else was racing through the ranks, a new state of nervousness so widespread it was almost palpable, a malaise that for some was translated into a little dance on the spot indicating that some Grade Fours would be visiting the toilet before they went back to class, even if in theory it wasn't allowed.

Claude Lemieux crossed his arms the way his mother did when she was angry.

"Go ahead.... Say you want to get rid of me!"

"Sure, sure, right away, that's exactly what I want — to get rid of you! You're the worst pain in the rear. You turn everything into a tragedy! Instead of griping all the time, why not just study like everybody else?"

"I told you a hundred times, I haven't got the foggiest idea what it's all about! Don't make me say it again, we just talked about it: I DON'T UNDERSTAND A THING ABOUT FRENCH!"

"You speak it, why can't you learn how to write it?"

"I do, but it's full of mistakes! I write it the same way I hear it but I guess I don't hear it right, and it's not my fault!"

Just before his class turned in the direction of the main door, the fat woman's child took a last look at the window where he'd spied Frère Martial. It was empty.

Wound up like a toy that can't be stopped, Claude Lemieux kept up his whining.

"I'll have to repeat my year, then you'll be happy! Go ahead, start Grade Five all by yourself, I'll stay behind like a dog...."

Once again he was on the brink of tears and once again his friend felt like smacking him.

He knew where to aim and how, without using physical force, and he did it — with an indifference that surprised even him.

"I don't think they'll make you repeat.... The Grade Four teachers hate your guts...they'd do anything to push you into Grade Five...."

The response came suddenly, awkward and wet. Even the voice was different, transformed by emotion. The fat woman's child knew what was coming next but he didn't have time to clap his hand over his friend's mouth.

"I know everybody else hates me! But I thought you liked me!"

Shouts, whistles, mocking laughter, the brother's raised voice, the two columns of boys setting off in disarray.

Somebody pinched Claude Lemieux's behind and he howled. His suffering was met with snickers and grimaces. He wanted to die. This was the third time today. And it was only ten after ten.

Frère Martial spoke to him in a tone he hadn't heard before. He realized from the first words that Marcel's teacher was trying to minimize the importance of something that had happened during recess: The mouth spoke soothing words — Marcel was tired, he'd gone home, he'd probably be back this afternoon — but the eyes betrayed something else, a blend of compassion and concern. The fat woman's child asked if his cousin had vomited. The reply was evasive.

"No, no...well, not really.... He had a...a kind of dizzy spell, let's say, and I advised him to go home...."

That was all the fat woman's child had to hear; he turned on his heels and silently walked away. Above all he mustn't be late for the second time in one day. He'd invented a call of nature to escape from his classmates, and now he had to get back in his seat before Frère Robert started handing out the exam questions.

He felt nothing at the prospect of this first exam that had all the others terrified. Not because he was so sure of passing, but because everything that had transpired between Marcel and himself since morning had distracted him from what should have been the focus of his day: the big white stapled examination books the teacher was handing out with a mysterious expression, the questions to be read, weighed, analyzed, the answers to be formulated clearly and in fluid, elegant handwriting, the final re-reading — perhaps the most important step of all — when you need both an over-all view of your work and a keen eye alert to the smallest spelling mistake, the slightest malformed letter that could be mistaken for another one.

For a long time he had confused his p's and q's, his d's and b's, the tails that stand up and the tails that hang down as he called them, and his teachers had come up with some ingenious ploys to straighten him out: "*D* is the first letter in the word *dos*. And our back is behind us. So the bump in *d* is behind the tail. *B*, though, is the first letter in the word *bédaine*. And our belly is in front of us." And so forth. Even now near the end of Grade Four he was still asking himself, whenever he had to print a *d* or a *b*, where his back and where his belly were, and he wondered if he'd have to keep doing it for the rest of his life. He could see himself still doing it when he was as old as his parents and it depressed him. At least the trick worked though, and now he never made a mistake.

The thirty-one pupils in Grade Four C were sitting quietly with their hands flat on their desks — all but Claude Lemieux who was still dabbing at his eyes. Frère Robert was writing something on the black-board. His new stick of chalk screeched and several youngsters winced.

The fat woman's child slipped into his seat with-out attracting the teacher's attention. Had Marcel really gone home at the risk of being scolded by his mother, or was he hiding out in his enchanted forest where once again he could forget everything? He told himself it was his duty to take a look at the front yard of 1474 Gilford on his way home, but he knew he wouldn't be brave enough, and once again he'd have to cover up for his cousin's flight. He felt tired and helpless. If Marcel was going to start having fits at school, word would travel quickly and smear the whole family, like everything else that happened to him. After the first few times Marcel had been called "pigeon" the whole family soon become "the pigeon family," and when his cousin was transferred to the supplementary class he started getting funny looks too, as if he were automatically being branded as someone to be avoided, even though he was at the head of his class. Were they going to start imitating Marcel's fits now, grotesquely mimicking the poor little body contorted by his illness, were they going to offer him a wooden spoon whenever he lost his temper or showed signs of impatience? Luckily there were just two more days of school and the students had other fish to fry.

Now Frère Robert had turned to face them. On the board, in blue chalk, he had written: *Fais ce que doigt.* He asked:

"Who can correct the mistake I put in that sentence?"

The fat woman's child shrugged.

"Look, that's really easy...."

Not one hand went up.

Frère Robert did his best to hide his disappointment.

"But it's easy. Just read what I wrote...."

Nothing.

He sighed, clasping his hands behind his back which was sagging slightly.

"Surely one of you.... You really can't see?"

Claude Lemieux timidly held up one finger and the fat woman's child rolled his eyes. *That's it, now he's going to be a martyr and make a fool of himself....*

Frère Robert seemed surprised.

"Go ahead, Lemieux, why is it so easy...."

Claude Lemieux stood up in the aisle, cleared his throat and said:

"I think there ought to be an *s* on *doigt*...."*

No reaction, not even a laugh. Frère Robert felt like jumping out the window. Couldn't *any* of them see a mistake as big as a house? In desperation he asked the fat woman's child, who usually did so well in French:

"Can't you see the mistake? I find that hard to believe!"

He'd wanted to make a joke of it, to lighten the atmosphere a little before exams started, but here he was once again facing the hopeless ignorance of his class. Had he really wasted an entire year trying to instill in them some basic notions about their language? And what had they been thinking about for the past four years? He often heard them say things like: "French is so boring!" "It's too complicated, I can't understand it...." "Why do there have to be so many words.... We don't need them all...."; and he'd reply with all the patience he could muster, explaining that French wasn't boring, on the contrary it was a fascinating language they should be proud of, that the rules might seem complicated at first but it would get easier as they came to understand them, that words used well are wonderful things...only to see them yawn in his face, or to realize they'd stopped listening ages ago. So why was he surprised at the inability of thirty students to spot such a glaring mistake? That was what he was asking himself as he waited for an answer from the fat woman's child, who was taking his time.

---

* "Fais ce que dois" — "Do what you must" — is the motto of the newspaper *Le Devoir*. "Doigt" means "finger."

The boy, who was in no mood to be given a hard time by his classmates, to be called a brown-noser or teacher's pet, decided to take a roundabout route to show the teacher he knew where the mistake was without actually having to say so.

"We're too nervous before our exam to understand a play on words like that."

He emphasized *play on words* to show the teacher he was well aware there was one, but Frère Robert reacted badly.

"Don't start telling me what to do in my class! You think you're smarter than the others, do you? Is that it? When I ask you a question I want a straight answer; never mind the parables."

Some laughter. The fat woman's child lowered his head. This really was not his day.

Furious, Frère Robert turned and grabbed the stack of exam questions from his desk. He took a few seconds before speaking to the class again.

"I don't know if it's worth the trouble of giving you these exam questions."

He slammed the sheets onto the first desk in front of him, Michel Daniel's.

"I've read these. They're pretty hard."

There were cries of protest and Claude Lemieux pulled the sopping handkerchief from his shirt pocket where it had already started leaving doubtful marks.

"You have exactly one hour. When you finish, give me your sheet and go home. This afternoon you'll have your Mathematics and Geography exams. And four more on Monday! You're going to have your work cut out for you!"

Just then there was a knock at the door. It was Frère Martial. The fat woman's child felt his heart leap up in his chest which was suddenly too small to contain it. That was it, now it would all come out; first the class, then the school and then the whole parish were going to know; they'd treat him like a sick person too...he'd end up like his cousin, the stupid pigeon, in the supplementary class, making stupid drawings all day long! Once again he flew out the window. Peter Pan executed a few handsprings in front of the school, then shot into the clouds like an arrow. Montreal receded into the distance forever, *Ah yes! forever.... I'm never coming back here! Ever! If only I can find it, find Peter Pan's Never Neverland, I swear I'll....*

When he came back to himself there was a set of exam questions on his desk. He looked up. Frère Robert was gazing at him very strangely, but with no animosity. He looked down at the sheet of paper...and couldn't understand a single word.

Perhaps it was a relief in the end. But his relief had an aftertaste of regret. He had gone into the enchanted forest by himself for the first time in a long while, which was obviously a victory, but something, a second of inattention, a momentary distraction had robbed him of the *freedom to choose* to push open the gate, to set one foot in front of the other and walk over the first bleeding hearts: Instead he found himself crouching in the centre of this yard he'd so often fled to without really wanting to, and that was frustrating.

When he'd left the school he knew he wouldn't go straight home; his mother could probably tell from his face what had happened and he was afraid of her reaction, even if his aunt was there to protect him. Not that Albertine would beat him, no, she rarely laid a hand on him, especially since he'd been a good inch taller than her for months now, but her insults and threats were as effective as blows: She knew where to strike and how hard, and how long to let her promises of punishments hang in the air; her verve was inexhaustible when it was time to humiliate her son. He felt too weak to put up with that.

And so he'd hung around for a while in the garden behind the Saint-Stanislas presbytery, surrounded by the last dandelions, reliving with horror the scene that had just been played out, blaming himself because he couldn't prevent the fit or feel it coming soon enough to ask to leave the room.... Though his cousin had said that morning that his eyes were yellow.... He picked a dandelion and wondered if his eyes were turning such a violent yellow or if, as his sister Thérèse had yelled at him one day, they were going to turn that dried mustard colour he hated so much. "Your eyes look so hot we could use them for a mustard plaster!"

And then, with no transition, he was standing outside 1474 Gilford — he didn't remember leaving the presbytery garden or crossing the street — and, also with no transition, he regained consciousness amid the smell of cat pee and the shifting shadows that made spots of sunlight dance on his arms and legs. So he hadn't decided to come back to the enchanted forest, his body had brought him here. It was the first time he'd been absent for so long while he was moving — it usually only happened in his head when he was resting, or dreaming when he was wide awake; people called that daydreaming and his aunt had told him it was normal, everybody does it, it's good for the imagination — and that had shaken him: He knew about sleepwalking, his mother did it sometimes when she was overtired, but he hadn't known you could sleepwalk when you're awake and that bothered him. "If I had one of those daydreams when I'm walking it could be dangerous! I could get run over! And on top of my confusions, it's not fair!"

But he was here in the heart of his invented forest, which was the main thing. He'd felt right away that tremendous sense of comfort at being alone, the precious certainty that nobody could find him, an unimaginable source of daydreaming hidden in some harmless, second-rate plants between a worm-eaten balcony and a rusted-out fence. The world was his now, with all its hidden forces, its incomprehensible barbarity, its Cold War, its atom bomb, its bleeding sunsets, his mean mother, his goddamn sickness — and he was going to run it! He was going to bring order to it, stir things up to suit him, remodel it and triumph as a creator who was aware of his own importance and proud of his genius.

He always began by dealing with his mother. That was easier, more gratifying too. Once she'd been liquidated the rest of the world would follow easily. After all, what's a Cold War or the atom bomb, both so remote and impossible to imagine, next to a mother who was there all the time and so much more threatening? He pictured himself sneaking up to the bed where she was fast asleep, snoring in that ugly way, yes, it would be a lot more interesting if she was snoring, he saw himself with a softly flaming match, bringing it close to her greying hair....

But then an automatic motion demolished his barely formed dream. He held out his left arm for Duplessis, his source of life, his inspiration, his love, his consolation in adversity, that mass of warm fur who had helped him get through everything for ten years now.... But there was nothing left of Duplessis — or so little. So little.

Marcel's scream was so violent, he hit his head against the brick wall of the house.

Anyone passing by who heard that cry would have plugged his ears and run away, thinking he had heard the dying of a child.

With a snap of her wrist, Albertine was sprinkling the laundry she'd spread over one end of the dining-room table they used as an ironing board. Then she held the iron near her cheek to test its heat, and finally set it down precisely on a shirt cuff, a skirt hem or a handkerchief. Steam rose into the room. At the other end of the table the fat woman was sorting clothes into two piles: her family's on one side, Albertine's on the other. She knew every piece of clothing in the household and sometimes amused herself by chanting the owner's names: "Gabriel, Albertine, Gabriel, Philippe, me, me, Albertine, Marcel..." which of course got on Albertine's nerves till she barked: "Keep it down, I can hardly hear the radio!" A soap opera was detailing its tribulations on the airwaves of CKAC and they stirred Albertine far more than the troubles of her own family. Yvette Brind'Amour had just lost a child, or Marjolaine Hébert a husband, and she reacted more keenly to them than to Marcel's latest lunacy or the marital problems of Thérèse who'd got married a few months earlier. She harassed Marcel and yelled insults at Thérèse on the phone, but she wept over the heartbreaking events in programmes like "Je vous ai tant aimé" or "Vie de femme."

The house smelled of Friday: Besides the steam from Albertine's ironing, eggs in white sauce were simmering on the coal stove. The two boys would turn up their noses and make a face when they came home for lunch. Marcel would settle for playing with his food and the fat woman's child would soak his bread in the sauce, careful to avoid picking up even a crumb of egg. The two women, though, would tuck into it with gusto, give themselves second helpings and scold their sons for not appreciating how good it was. Good for their health and good to eat. Marcel would end up eating bread spread with ketchup or mustard while his cousin, to please his mother, would force himself to chew on a chalky egg yolk that would make him sick to his stomach.

The soap opera was nearly over. It would be followed by another one very much like it, with the same actors in roles not all that different repeating the same inane remarks in the same tone of voice....

The fat woman pushed the pile of her family's clothes towards Albertine, who was wiping her face with her forearm.

"Be careful, Gabriel ripped the bottom of his blue shirt.... I don't know if we've got any navy thread.... If we don't we'll have to send the boy to Marie-Sylvia's...."

Albertine picked up the shirt and tried to find the tear.

"Anyway, Marie-Sylvia's out of everything but penny candy and shoelaces. We'll have to go to Schiller's."

The fat woman tried not to smile. For a while now Albertine would use any excuse for going to Schiller's store at the corner of Fabre and Mont-Royal. The owner had a weakness for her, he didn't hide it, in fact he'd almost spoken out a few weeks before. Albertine wasn't interested — her husband had turned her off men for good, as she'd been shouting from the rooftops for years — but Mr. Schiller's repeated attentions, the bargains he gave her, the interest suggested by every smile, were very flattering. She'd walk into the store with perfect posture, a mischievous smile on her lips (she who never smiled), asked for what she wanted in a voice that wasn't hers, using words that weren't hers either, then she would leave, transformed, light, and almost pleasant. It left her illuminated for several hours, to the joy of the rest of the family. No reprimands for Marcel, less growling at the other members of the household and sometimes even a more carefully prepared meal.

Only once had her sister-in-law referred to Mr. Schiller, actually calling him Albertine's admirer, but the other woman's reaction had been so spiteful, so hostile, that now if his name came up the fat woman merely smiled — a smile that was very explicit and filled with insinuations, to which Albertine, needless to say, didn't dare react.

"Fine, you can go after lunch. I'll finish the ironing. Meanwhile, I think we can take a little break."

Albertine settled in the old chair that had belonged to her mother, Victoire. It was a rocking chair that hadn't rocked for ages because after years of use the wood, so beautiful and solid when Josaphat-le-violon had chopped, cut, and assembled it in Duhamel around the turn of the century, was now so worn after years of scraping and jostling that it was dangerous. For obvious reasons the fat woman had given up sitting in it years before, but pigheaded Albertine had decided she wasn't at risk and she'd flop into it quite brutally under her sister-in-law's horrified gaze, to listen to her soap operas by day and her quiz shows by night.

When she wasn't working she would look at the radio while listening to it, exactly as if she could see what she was hearing. She could gaze for hours at the little yellow light that marked the stations, coming closer if the action was heating up or if she thought she knew the answer to a question. During "Tentez votre chance," a special favourite of hers, she would sometimes put both hands on the huge speaker, press her lips against the dial and shriek the answer, calling the competitor every name in the book. When the rest of the family teased her, she would say: "I know they can't hear me, I'm not that stupid, I just like doing it, it makes me feel good!" After a brief silence she'd mutter between her teeth: "Besides, you never know...."

Albertine had been "watching" the sufferings of Antoinette Giroux for several minutes when the fat woman remembered an article she'd seen in *La Presse* the day before. She picked up the paper which was lying on a chair waiting to be used to wrap potato peels and easily found the article, accompanied by a huge photograph that had fascinated her. She waited till the heart-rending scene was over before offering her sister-in-law the paper.

"Here, read this, it's interesting...."

Albertine was noisily blowing her nose into a cotton handkerchief. Antoinette Giroux had just kicked out Albert Duquesne and it broke her heart — not because of any fondness for the character he played but because she liked his voice.

"You know I never read the papers. They're just full of nonsense...."

"Just read this big article, here...."

"I don't feel like it.... Tell me, it'll be faster...."

Sighing, the fat woman pulled a straight chair

close to her sister-in-law's, picked up the paper again, and folded it in four so Albertine could see the photo.

"Look.... See that, they call it a television...."

Albertine glanced at it indifferently.

"Looks like an electric oven."

In view of Albertine's lack of enthusiasm, the fat woman decided to speak for herself. The article had made a great impression on her and she'd been musing about it since the day before.

"Apparently these things are wonderful...like having the movies in your own house.... They come right out and say so, see, here.... It's like a radio but it's more than a radio. It's a radio with pictures! You can see the picture at the same time you're listening to your programme.... Like the movies.... Except it's never in colour."

Albertine had frowned while her sister-in-law was speaking, then she held the picture up to her nose.

"Come off it! They don't know what they're talking about!"

Happy she'd finally roused Albertine's curiosity, the fat woman moved closer to her and bent over the newspaper.

"No, no, it's true, look! They did tests and everything. Some people in the States even have one in their house! What do you think about that!"

"You can listen to the programme and see what's going on at the same time?"

"That's right!"

"I could never do that!"

"What do you mean, you couldn't?"

"Well, I'm used to just listening.... I couldn't do both things at once."

"You nitwit, when you go to the movies you look

and listen at the same time and you don't have any trouble understanding."

"I know, but at the movies I'm used to it. And I don't do my mending and my knitting while I'm watching! I pay to go to the movies and I eat my chips and drink my Coke! Anyway, don't you remember the trouble I had getting used to it when the talkies came!"

"Bartine! You were just a little girl back then, we didn't even know each other!"

"Well it was hard for me anyway! I'd got used to reading in between the pictures so when the sound came, I couldn't figure it out! Everything happened too fast at the same time! And I thought it made a lot of noise...."

"That may be, but you still got used to it...."

"It took a long time! And I don't feel like starting over again.... No, I like my radio just the way it is...."

"That's fine, but when you listen to the radio you're always looking at the dial.... Wouldn't you rather have something real to look at, like the movies?"

"I wouldn't understand a thing! There's way too much noise in this house! And too much light! We'd have to turn off all the lights to watch, like in the movies! And how'll we get around the house if it's pitch black and we can't see a thing?"

The fat woman sighed impatiently.

"When you decide you don't want to understand something...."

"I do so understand! Why do you say I don't understand? I just don't want any movies here, that's all! I'll never have one in my house, get it, never!"

"I didn't say I wanted one in the house, they probably cost a small fortune. I just wanted to tell you about it! Don't you want to have some idea about what's going on in the world?"

"What's the good of knowing there's people in the States with movies in their houses if I don't want it? Anyway, the movies are way too big! The thing would take up a whole wall. We'd have to put the chairs across the street to see anything, there isn't enough room in here! Who wants to go blind just so they can watch Antoinette Giroux cry? I can imagine that by myself!"

"Who said a television takes up a whole wall! Where'd you come up with that one? It's small. Just seventeen inches!"

"Seventeen inches! You wouldn't see a thing! They'll be the size of my hand! We'd have to stick our noses right against the picture! I'd just as soon not see them!"

The fat woman picked up the newspaper, got to her feet, and dropped it on the table.

"Okay, okay, forget I said anything. Never mind."

Albertine turned up the radio.

"We'll talk about it some other time. Right now 'Les Joyeux Troubadours' are going to start, and Estelle Caron promised yesterday she'd sing 'Plaisir d'amour'...."

She turned abruptly before her sister-in-law could react.

"No, I wouldn't want to see Estelle Caron sing 'Plaisir d'amour!' Because while she's singing 'Plaisir d'amour,' I'm going to go and stir my white sauce!"

On the radio the joyous troubadours were already bellowing: "Don't believe everything you hear, that's the way to stay happy...."

More and more she felt as if she were living with what she called a walking safe whenever she thought of Albertine. She often talked about it with her husband, Gabriel, who told her Albertine had always been withdrawn, mule-headed, and grouchy, and the main thing was not to try to change her. Victoire, their mother, used to try; with the patience of an angel she'd used affection and persuasion, but even as a child Albertine had resisted any approach, avoided getting close to anyone — her mother, her brothers, her sister Madeleine, her few girlfriends; instead she stayed by herself in her corner, judging others and herself, obstinately defending her own ideas, especially when she was in the wrong. Her family had very early started calling her "the mule" and the name had stuck.

An unhappy marriage and two difficult children were all it took to make her bitter, impatient, a total mess; and more recently a new feeling she'd tried at first to repress, to no avail — jealousy. It had wormed its way into her heart when she saw the enduring happiness of the fat woman and Gabriel, their complicity that had lasted now for more than twenty years — their courage in the face of poverty, the likely success of their three children: Richard, the oldest, who would start teaching in September and who revered his parents; Philippe, always scattered, always a joker, who skipped from job to job but was never short of money and somehow always got along; and the baby of the family who was always at the head of his class, his mother's darling, too quiet for her liking, but she knew he was bright and she was well aware of his affection for her, even though she did everything to curb it, discourage it.

When she thought about Thérèse on the arm of the worm she'd married even though she didn't love him, just to get out of the house and aggravate her mother, about her escapades on the Main that usually ended violently, about the alcoholism that was insidiously marking her features; when she watched Marcel growing up with his strange expressions and his waking dreams, so agitated it was driving her crazy and so unpredictable she was beginning to be afraid of him, a big kid who would soon become a man — but what kind of man, for the love of God, what kind of a backward child who would constantly need protection even while she was protecting herself from him; when she added it all up, the tiny pile of never-ending miseries, the ridiculous sum of her pointless words and deeds, the insignificance of her life, she would hide her head in her pillow and howl for hours: in the middle of the afternoon when there was nothing to do till supper and the fat woman had disappeared into one of those goddamn books it was so hard to get her out of, in the middle of the night when Marcel was moaning and grinding his teeth and she told herself it was her fault he wasn't normal, that she never should have had children, she didn't deserve them, and now she was being punished....

Sometimes in the movies too, when the French kiss between Ingrid Bergman and her partner lasted too long, or when Esther Williams jumped from a helicopter into a coloured swimming pool, Albertine would open her purse, take out her little cotton handkerchief, sniff, blow her nose, cough, sob uncontrollably, eyes glued to the screen where an inaccessible world seemed to be mocking her, sneering at her, at her mediocrity, at her little square of cotton and her puffy eyes. The people sitting next to her, who had never seen anyone cry during an Esther Williams movie, would move discreetly or nudge one another and laugh....

So why bring all that into the house in the form of a radio you can look at, why let your privacy be invaded by a world that was too beautiful, that you'd never in a million years have access to? She'd rather die! Or once again be seen as an ignoramus by her sister-in-law, whose compassion felt so insulting.

She would stay with her nose against the yellow dial of her radio and the movies would remain inside, where they belonged: at the Passe-Temps, the Bijou and, on special occasions, the Saint-Denis.

The fat woman had retired to her bedroom right after Jean-Maurice Bailly's first joke. She had heard the safe door slam shut and she knew Albertine had double-locked herself inside and would be incommunicado for the rest of the day. Anyway, she was in no mood to watch her sister-in-law listen imperturbably to all the jokes and carryings-on during the next half-hour of the "Joyeux Troubadours." She had asked her once why she didn't laugh when it was funny and Albertine had replied: "Who says I don't laugh?"

She had brought *La Presse* and now she spread it over the pink chenille bedspread that was threadbare, especially where every morning and every night she sat her broad rear end when she got dressed or undressed. Gabriel often observed, smiling: "You're hard on that poor chenille," to which she replied in the same tone: "If we could afford satin, my rear end would be just as hard on it, only it would cost a lot more!"

She bent over the illustration again and read the description of the set, the brand-name, Admiral, and the price, exorbitant.

All the knowledge in the world was there, she knew it was. Movies in your own house? More than movies, a visual radio that would cover the news everywhere in the world exactly when it was happening; a book open on the universe; a window you'd want to climb through, that would look out on absolutely everything. All that in their house! She ran her hand over the greyish screen as if she were smoothing a piece of fine cloth or a child's cheek. Something new was growing in her, a determination she'd never felt before, a need of such colossal force she knew it was definitive and that she'd never be free of it. She had managed to bury the dreams of Acapulco that had haunted her for so long with the appearance of this new child who had so changed her life ten years ago, but that hunger, that rage, she knew were irremediable — and she knew that if she didn't satisfy them she would die. She wanted that window on the world at any price, and she would have it no matter what it cost and no matter what her miserable sister-in-law had to say.

On the other side of her bedroom door, which opened onto the dining room, the safe had come out of her room and was starting to set the table while Gérard Paradis and Estelle Caron performed in some supremely ridiculous sketch. She felt a pang at the thought of the first exam her son had just written.

He looked at the sheet of paper as if he'd never seen one before in his life. A large white square covered with letters that formed words, words that formed sentences, sentences that ordinarily should have been answers to the questions printed there in black. But he wasn't sure. He had answered every question, he knew he had because the white spaces below the questions were filled with his handwriting, which was rather ugly and less controlled than usual, less aware that it was going to be read by an inquisitive eye on the lookout for any awkwardness, any imperfection. He'd lose some marks for his handwriting then. But would he win any for his answers?

He had watched himself writing as if someone else were leaning over his own shoulder. It was the second time this kind of thing had happened since morning, this ability to come out of himself and watch himself act, and he wondered if it could be the beginning of a disturbance like his cousin's. He had watched himself write then but without really registering what he was writing, as if his hand was independent of his will and hadn't been following the orders of his brain. But how could his hand write the answers to questions his brain didn't understand? He didn't even know if the exam had really been hard, though the teacher had just said it was!

During the hour that had just gone by his heart had taken up too much room in his chest; he could feel it pounding in his temples; he was sure the rest of the class could hear it. The class was one enormous heart whose beating could be felt by the whole school, the whole parish. The entire city of Montreal could hear the panic that his heart betrayed, and was spitefully enjoying it. From Longue-Pointe to Sainte-Geneviève people knew that a little boy in the parish of Saint-Stanislas who usually did very well in French had just failed his exam and now all he could do was die and wipe out his disgrace.

He ran his hand over the questions, from top to bottom, as if smoothing out non-existent wrinkles. Only five minutes till the bell. This was the moment when he should have re-read his answers quickly, correcting some poorly closed *s*'s or an *o* that could be taken for an *a*, but his right hand kept making this ridiculous move he couldn't understand, automatic and uncontrollable, continuing against his will, and that he doubted he could ever stop.

Some of his classmates had already got up, most of them pathetic, lowering their heads and dropping their exams on Frère Robert's desk, then leaving the classroom as if it were a prison, relieved to be free of a burden that was much too heavy for them. Some had even given a real cry of deliverance that had made the teacher frown.

Running feet could be heard in the corridor. From every classroom on this floor exhausted children emerged who only wanted to forget the hideous hour they'd just spent and not think about those to come this afternoon.

The fat woman's child realized that his hand had stopped smoothing his exam. Someone in the room upstairs had just dropped something heavy on the floor and he looked up at the ceiling. A small brownish spot that looked like a hole he'd never seen before drew his attention.

A hole in the ceiling of his classroom....

He saw himself on a pitch-black night kneeling on the floor of the classroom above, bent over the hole he'd just made with a brace and bit, a bottle of ink, Waterman's South Sea Blue, in his hand. And he wondered how many bottles of Waterman's South Sea Blue it would take to fill the whole classroom. And how much time. A week? A month? All summer? What a neat arithmetic problem! Interesting too, for once!

He could see the classroom floor take on the colour of the south seas, see the ink spread from the cloakroom to the raised platform for the teacher's desk, see it slowly rising, bottle after bottle, licking the feet of the desks, coming to the bottom of the big bronze radiators, their seats, the blackboard; he watched the brushes floating on the tide of South Sea Blue, the white chalk swallowed by the turquoise forever, saw the hermetically-closed windows hold back the liquid that became transparent as it coated the glass. He saw the white globes of the ceiling fixtures float for a moment, then sink; and the beautiful green light they would produce in the heart of his sea. He saw himself just as the last bottle of Waterman's South Sea Blue caused the little hole in the floor to overflow, so he'd be absolutely sure that Grade Four C had just disappeared forever, drowning not only the memory but the very existence of a failed French exam. And he smiled ecstatically.

All at once the clock burst into his dream. The classroom was drained of its turquoise liquid. The examination, failed or not, still existed. He looked

down at the sheet of paper. He saw the word "object."
Object? What's an object? Then it all came back to
him. Subject, verb, object. Direct and indirect. He read
some of the questions. He understood them all. But it
was too late. Frère Robert was already holding out his
hand.

"You're dawdling this morning. Is everything all
right?"

Of course Claude Lemieux was waiting for him at the schoolyard gate, squatting on the bottom step, panic written across his face. He was still wiping his eyes when the fat woman's child came out.

"Are you crying again! That must be the twelfth time today! Don't you ever dry up?"

Claude Lemieux stuffed his handkerchief back in his damp shirt pocket. The fat woman's child sat down beside him. He wasn't hungry. He didn't feel like going home. He could have stayed there, burning in the sun, till someone came for him, his frantic mother or one of his angry brothers, until they told him: "It's not so serious, failing an exam. Not with your average. They'll think you were sick.... We'll explain, they'll understand.... Just pull yourself together for the Math exam this afternoon...."

He hadn't realized Claude Lemieux had come up to him, the way he always did when he was "feeling nice," as he put it. But the fat woman's child was in no mood for Claude to feel nice and he pushed him away.

"How come you're pushing me? That must be the twelfth time today!"

A group of Grade Nine boys came outside, swearing, calling the brothers terrible names. The exam was too hard: they'd never in a million years understand the first thing about the imperfect subjunctive, so why did the teachers keep pushing it at them? Why force them to learn verb tenses they'd never use, because only pansies talked like that? The only thing they'd ever remembered about all that, because it made them laugh, was that the imperfect subjunctive of the verb "savoir," which they were never asked for as a matter of fact, sounded just like "suck."

They had even forgotten to bug the two Grade Four kids, Banana Split and Frère Robert's pet, who were lingering on the cement steps.

Sighing, the fat woman's child stood up.

"Guess we better get moving if we want to come back after lunch...."

Claude Lemieux copied him, even down to the sigh, and stood on his left.

"You didn't even console me for flunking my exam...."

His classmate smiled in spite of himself. His friend's monstrous self-absorption had always fascinated him. Claude always brought everything around to himself, without thinking; it had become second nature with him, deeply anchored in everything he did, a fundamental need, probably a way to increase his importance in his own eyes since most of the time nobody even noticed him. He had the vanity of those who are boring.

The fat woman's child shrugged, then he kicked at a stone that flew off in the wrong direction.

"Don't worry, I flunked mine too."

Without taking the time to be surprised, Claude Lemieux turned towards him.

"That's impossible! Isn't it? Are you sure? Want me to console you?"

How about that, a burst of generosity.... The other boy grasped his shoulder, gently pulled him against his own hip. Claude Lemieux sighed contentedly as he wrapped his arm around his friend's waist.

"I like it when you're nice to me like that."

So that was it.... He wasn't being generous after all, it was just a way to wheedle some affection....

They walked in silence across the yard behind the church, one boy perfectly happy to be holding close to him the person he cherished most in the world after his mother, the other deep in his own disgrace, and they were almost at 1474 Gilford when Claude Lemieux whispered in his friend's ear:

"I know you didn't fail your exam, you just said you did to make me happy!"

Didn't that take the cake! The fat woman's child felt like strangling his friend. He saw him turn red and then blue in his hands; quivering veins stood out on his forehead, his eyes pleaded, but he kept squeezing till his own fingers turned white, then all at once the other boy stopped breathing and he flung the body away like a sated vampire. With a roar of relief he ran to hide — but where?

They were at the enchanted forest now and Claude Lemieux was saying: "How come you're staring like that? You never saw bleeding hearts before? They come out every spring and they last till July.... My mother won't let me touch them.... She says...." He hadn't had time to complete his sentence when his friend shoved him, hard.

"You can go now. Go home and eat your lunch. I'll see you at a quarter to one at the bottom of my stairs."

Claude, who had almost lost his balance, pulled

himself up on tiptoes. It was a sign he was about to throw a tantrum.

"You're mean! What's wrong with you all of a sudden? You got no business shoving me like that. First you're nice, then you shove me away like I don't exist! You're going to end up all alone one of these days, you know! I could get fed up!"

The fat woman's child had heard this litany hundreds of times; he turned around. He couldn't hear Claude Lemieux who he knew would be running away, crying, when he realized he didn't have his full attention any more, but he'd be back in an hour, sweet as sugar.

He heard a rustling from the enchanted forest. Someone was there, Marcel most likely, whose mere presence was accomplishing if not an actual miracle then a moment of grace, a privileged moment of surprising sweetness, that was expressed as a murmuring in the branches, as if a wind from inside the bushes were trying to escape. It was a dream, yet it was all very real.

On this glorious summer afternoon the bees were buzzing, the crickets were announcing rather hysterically that the next day would be just as beautiful, just as singable as this one, a flock of birds was preparing for a wedding later on that evening, a little breeze was wafting everywhere, brushing against your legs like a hungry cat, the air smelled of cooling raspberry jam and of fresh corn simmering in water with a little milk added to keep it tender; a perfect day, in August perhaps, and it was coming directly from the clump of bleeding hearts. It was Marcel's work, and the fat woman's child wanted to know how he went about inventing all this beauty.

But something held him back. As he approached the metal fence he realized that Marcel was asleep, that this perfect August day had been born of his cousin's sleep, and he didn't want to "violate" such an intimate moment. Their great-uncle Josaphat-le-violon, brother of their grandmother Victoire, often used to tell them you must never look at somebody who's sleeping, that it's a violation (for years all the children in the family thought that "violation" had something to do with playing the violin like their uncle, and the fat woman's child still thought so), and that it can bring bad luck. He had told them: "When a person's asleep it's the only time he's really all alone, so you mustn't disturb him. See, he's fixing everything that's wrong in his life."

He didn't want to bother Marcel, most of all he didn't want to keep him from fixing what was wrong in his life, but...he *wanted* some part of this marvellous day, a small, even microscopic piece of the happiness that such a beautiful dream must bring. He dreamed beautiful dreams too; but though there was always some hitch in a beautiful dream, even the most wonderful, this one seemed to be...perfect. Simply perfect.

But was Marcel really asleep? He remembered what had happened before in the enchanted forest, when neither he nor his cousin was asleep, and he thought that maybe Marcel was wide awake while he dreamed such a beautiful, desirable dream, and that maybe disturbing somebody who is dreaming while wide awake wasn't so serious.... He pushed open the gate, frowning when it creaked. He bent over slightly. It was very dark in there. He remembered the smell of cat pee and the roughness of the brick wall. But he crouched down anyway, got onto his hands and knees, advancing cautiously.

Marcel was asleep. He was lying on his back, his right arm seemed to be wrapped around something or somebody that wasn't there, and there was an ecstatic smile on his lips. Marcel smiled so rarely in everyday life that the fat woman's child stood frozen there watching him for a few seconds. It was so beautiful! He came closer to his cousin's face. A sweetness had fallen, fallen *onto* Marcel's features. It didn't seem to have come from inside but to have settled there, like an exquisitely delicate mask. Shadows cast by the bleeding hearts shifted across it, soothing his forehead and erasing any trace of anxiety. The sleeping Marcel was a different person from the waking one. Asleep, Marcel was a Sleeping Beauty who must not be wakened, not even after a hundred years, because the sleeping Marcel was happy. That Marcel didn't need to attend a supplementary class, no one would ever call him "pigeon," no, his friends — proud to be his friends — would simply call him by his name, biting into it, because merely saying it would give them so much pleasure. This Marcel was the real one, he realized all at once, and he wanted to know who exactly he was.

And the violation?

A dilemma.

He crossed his arms, thought about it for a few seconds.

He quickly concluded that he must not disturb his cousin. But the temptation was too strong.

He laid his hand on his cousin's forehead.

Immediately a cloud of birds exploded into the enchanted forest; they came from Marcel's brow, from his head, they ran down his arm like an electrical charge, played in his hair, flying, cheeping, forming a mixture of colours the like of which he'd never seen; it was every hue at once but he couldn't have named even one, so new did they appear. So *that* was the rustling. Wings. Thousands of wings. Fanning Marcel's brow while he slept. He looked on, thrilled, unable to follow the flight of a single bird but very skilled at sensing the throbbing of the flock because it formed a complete entity.

With a single cry of warning or terror, the flight of birds burst like a bubble, flowed into colours even more demented, and disappeared.

Then a magnificent tiger-striped cat sprang into the forest, panting, agitated, and breathless, its teeth bared and so absorbed in the chase that it was comical. It was a treat to watch the huge alley cat — he was in such fine fettle, so muscular you were sure he must be a local terror; his muzzle was pink and moist, his whiskers just the right length, a thin black line emphasized the mouth so that he looked as if he was not so much smiling as actually laughing at you.

He didn't see the fat woman's child right away, and when he snarled, "Where the hell are they, I thought grabbing them would be a cinch!" the little boy jumped. The cat, sensing the movement, turned towards him. "What do you think you're doing? You aren't supposed to see me!" Then he noticed the boy's hand on Marcel's forehead. "Thief! Get away from him! You should be ashamed of yourself!" With arched back, tail an exclamation mark, claws out, he was preparing to charge. Frightened, Marcel's cousin pulled away his hand. Now there was nothing but darkness, bleeding hearts, the smell of cat pee. He thought the contact had been broken and he wanted to put his hand back on his cousin's forehead.

But Marcel was awake now. All at once his cares and misfortunes were visible on his face again. He blanched, his features drawn as if he'd been exercising hard. In a broken voice he pleaded:

"Don't steal my summer. Don't steal my cat. I can only see him when I'm dreaming now.... Let me keep him. Please, just let me sleep." He closed his eyes. The fat woman's child bent down very close to his face.

"You can't stay there. You have to come home and eat. Your mother'll be worried."

At the mention of his mother, Marcel scowled.

"Tell her...just tell her I stayed at school. Say I'll come right home after four. Say anything you want, but don't tell on me!"

A small laceration opened in the soul of the fat woman's child. At one and the same time, he felt Marcel's despair and his own jealousy. He'd have given everything just then, everything — his passion for books, his love for his parents, his privileges for coming first in class — if he could insinuate himself inside his cousin's head long enough for just one dream.

To see Duplessis again.

"So how'd it go this morning?" Claire Lemieux was stirring up a batter made of stale bread, milk, eggs, and a little too much vanilla that would go in the oven for the evening meal. Getting no answer, she left the kitchen, wiping her hands on an apron of dubious cleanliness. "I'm making bread pudding for supper, you like that!"

Claude had flopped onto his bed at the back of the bedroom they shared, for want of space. His mother came in and sat beside him. "It doesn't matter if you don't pass all your exams, Momma's got a nice surprise for you." Claude wiped his eyes that were red from the tears he'd been shedding since morning. "A surprise? What kind of surprise?"

Claire Lemieux had been preparing for this moment for some months now. With superhuman efforts, she had managed to hide from her son the plan she'd cooked up with her own mother, one she was sure would thrill him since he was crazy about both his grandmother and the country. Oh, there'd be some protests at first, maybe even a little tantrum, but after that he'd settle down. With her thumb she wiped the tear stains from her son's cheeks. "Next week, as soon as your exams are over, we're going away." Claude pulled back and leaned against the wall. "Go away? Where to?" His mother was wearing her "pleasant surprises" expression; her surprises were always amazing but not necessarily pleasant, and he'd been wary of them since he was a small child.

"We're going to Saint-Eustache, to Grandma's."

He should have been delighted. He was suspicious. He'd be glad to see his grandmother's little house again, with the lake nearby where he could go swimming, his bedroom, *his very own bedroom*, that looked out on a little yard his grandmother called the garden because of the puny gladioli she grew there; he smelled the aroma of apple pie that seemed permanently attached to the kitchen; the cool, fresh sheets that gave off a perfume he'd always associated with the holidays: it smelled like Christmas and Easter and of course presents; but there was something, an unfamiliar excitement, in his mother's eyes, in the fold of her mouth too, and even in the way her hand moved along the edge of the bed that didn't really hide a state of agitation he hadn't seen before, that stopped him from jumping for joy as he usually did whenever Claire told him they were going to Saint-Eustache.

"Aren't you glad?"

Then he understood the real reason for his concern. She'd said his exam results weren't important. A tide of blood came too quickly, making his head spin; he realized he was scared.

"Why'd you say it doesn't matter if I fail my exams?"

She put her arms around him, lifted him up, and waltzed him around the room. He hadn't seen her in such a state since the death of his father, Heartless Hector, whom they'd hated so much and whose death the whole street had celebrated because he'd been such a miserable, lazy, good-for-nothing.

"Are we just going for a few weeks like we always do?"

She rubbed her nose against his as she used to do when he was a baby.

"No!"

He struggled, freed himself, retreated to his bed again.

"Don't say we're going for the whole summer! I already told you, I don't want to go for the whole summer! There's hardly any kids on Grandma's street, there's nobody to play with! All my friends are here! I want to be here with them!"

His mother's smile didn't disappear and that frightened him even more.

She stuffed her hands in her apron pockets.

"Still haven't figured it out, eh?"

He had, but a deliberate block kept him from putting into thoughts what he'd sensed from his mother's first words. He lifted the bedspread, burrowed under the cotton blanket, and hid his head under the pillow.

His mother sat down next to him and kneaded his bum the way she did on bad mornings when she had to beg him to get up.

"You'll make other friends.... The school in Saint-Eustache has lots of kids! I've already registered you. Your Grandma knows the principal.... You'll go right into Grade Five! Won't that be nice? You won't have to repeat Grade Four. And you'll love it in the country! You're such a puny little thing now. You'll get your strength back, you'll grow faster, you'll turn into a man!"

Claude leaped out of his bed, ran across their room and the hallway, opened the front door and tore down the outside stairs, screaming.

Claire Lemieux didn't move a hair. She'd been expecting his reaction and she took it with a grain of salt. In a few hours the tantrum would pass and Claude would realize the advantages of living in the country, she was sure of it.

She leaned against the wall and thought of what a deliverance her husband's death a few months earlier had been. A cancer, unexpected and merciless — too many cigarettes, too much fat, not enough exercise — a brief, violent agony, a hasty burial. Deliverance. Peace. She had just handed in her resignation at Giroux et Deslauriers where she'd been selling shoes for years and landed a job as a waitress in Saint-Eustache, right next to the church. She and her mother would bring up Claude all by themselves, with no men — that's right, no men! — and he'd become their pride, their reason for living.

Here, it would be too hard. And she'd had enough of Fabre Street, of the lack of privacy, the malicious gossip — everybody knew everything about everybody else and always minded everybody else's business — Claude's friends in particular, who she thought were peculiar because most of them had been born during the same summer as her son and their excessive complicity frightened her. She didn't like the fat woman's child, or the two Carmens, Carmen Ouimet and Carmen Brassard, or Jay-Pee Jodoin or Linda Lauzon, they were too noisy when you left them alone and too secretive when you told them to be quiet. The younger ones bothered her too: Manon Brassard, a pious little hypocrite who looked as if butter wouldn't melt in her mouth; the flock of little Jodoins who were more like gypsies than anything else; the little Lauzon boy who was always making faces. They lived in their own world, one that made her uncomfortable, and she wanted to remove her son from their influence.

She dreamed of the life awaiting her in Saint-Eustache, of the mild summer evenings, the beautiful winter nights.... The days would all resemble one another and she'd be able to drown in their harmony.

Squealing brakes, a scream. She thought she was going to die.

As he turned the corner of Fabre and Gilford, the fat woman's child could see Madame Lemieux beating her child right out on the street. She was doing it with a lot of energy and a lot of conviction and he could hear the blows raining down on his friend's neck, his shoulders, and his backside. The neighbours had come out on their balconies, and so had his mother and his aunt. A car had stopped near Claude and his mother and Marie-Sylvia was yelling from her steps, but you couldn't hear what she was saying over the child's cries.

The fat woman's child ran towards them as if he wanted to help Claude, but Madame Lemieux pointed to him and shrieked:

"It's all your fault! He was going to meet you! Can't you learn to leave that child alone!"

He stopped short ten steps away from them. The unfairness of her accusation paralyzed him. It was Claude who never left *him* in peace, who clung like a leech, not him! His friend was giving him his worst imploring look and it made him want to take over from Claude's mother.

Marie-Sylvia took advantage of the silence, one she knew would be of brief duration, to say: "I saw everything! Everything! He went across the street like a bat out of hell, without even looking for cars! He hasn't the faintest idea about how to behave! Like the whole lot of them! They're all the same! Can't keep still for a minute!"

Claire Lemieux, annoyed at this interference, turned towards the old woman.

"Listen, you, mind your own business! Have you ever had kids? Eh? You haven't, have you? So keep out of this! And instead of telling us how to bring them up you could quit selling those penny surprise bags that're going to poison them one of these days! If they can't keep still like you say, it's because of what you sell them! Stale candy that attacks their brains!"

Marie-Sylvia slammed the door of her restaurant after her final denunciation: "Says who? I don't want to see hide nor hair of them again! Ever! They can buy their surprise bags somewhere else! And you, you fanatic, don't you bother showing your face either!"

The fat woman's child had come a few steps closer. Claude trembled as he watched him approach. He could have touched him, consoled him as he did so often, but at the same time he felt like hitting him. He was always the same: He attracted as much contempt as pity. Simultaneously.

The fat woman called softly from the balcony: "Come on up, sweetheart, come home and eat. Let them straighten out their own affairs...."

And then all was silent. They formed a *tableau vivant* in the middle of the street: Madame Lemieux breathing fast like someone who wants to keep herself from crying; Claude was doubled over, afraid his mother would start hitting him again; the fat woman's child looking on glumly, not knowing whether to follow his mother's advice or stay and defend his friend;

the driver of the car that had almost run over Claude still leaning against his front fender, trembling and wiping his brow. The incident had ended without too much damage; the neighbours, somewhat disappointed, were going home to finish their lunch. Only the fat woman was still on the balcony, in her rocking chair. Her son knew that without even turning around to check.

Claire Lemieux broke the silence after she'd grabbed Claude by the arm. "Look here, son, I'm sorry. I know it wasn't your fault.... I was so upset...." And no one added anything else. Madame Lemieux didn't thank the driver for not killing her child and he got back into his car without another word. The fat woman's child climbed slowly up the outside staircase. The car drove away.

But just as he and his mother were going inside, Claude Lemieux turned and shouted across the street to his friend: "My mother's taking me away to Saint-Eustache forever! We'll never see each other again!"

"Why isn't he with you? Where is he this time?"

With his fork he mashed the pieces of egg into the white sauce, stirred it up, spread some on a slice of bread, and shut his eyes before he put the mixture in his mouth. It didn't taste as bad as he'd expected, but the pasty consistency was disgusting and he had trouble getting it down. His mother acted as if she didn't see a thing and swallowed a big forkful. He looked at her wide-eyed and perplexed, wondering if she really liked it or was just doing this to defy him. He dived back into his plate because his aunt had opened her mouth to say something.

"Answer me when I speak to you! I'm not your mother, they'll never give me a prize for patience!"

The fat woman gave her a look that was half-amused, half-severe.

"For heaven's sake Bartine! Let the child finish his meal! It's bad enough he doesn't like it, if he has to talk while he's eating he'll get sick for sure!"

He laid down his fork. "I'm not hungry anyway."

He saw his mother's face suddenly creased with concern, something that happened more and more often. She had trouble concealing her emotions: Her face would light up with joy and you wanted to hug her or share her happiness; bad news or some irritation would distort her features in a few seconds and guilt would grab you by the throat. You had to say no, no, that isn't true, I'm hungry, the egg sauce is delicious, everything's fine; but it was too late, she was speaking.

"You didn't say anything about your exam this morning. How was it?"

Should he tell the truth? ("I didn't understand a single question, I'm a moron, it's all Marcel's fault and his cat's and his enchanted forest's and that stupid disease of his; I couldn't concentrate, I flunked my exam and I'll flunk the others too because why should things get any better this afternoon, I'll have to repeat Grade Four....") Lie to her? ("It was easy, I finished before everybody else, the brother couldn't get over it, I can't wait for this afternoon, I can't wait for Monday.... I know I'll be one of the first three....")

"It was okay."

The answer had come out without his formulating it. He'd aimed at the extremes and landed in the middle. A remark that was meaningless, banal, neither happy nor sad, whereas actually everything was seething inside him and nothing would have been more comforting than a word from his mother or her hand on his brow.

"That doesn't tell me anything, 'okay'. Was it good or was it bad? What I want to know is, how was the exam?"

Albertine scraped her plate with her fork.

"You're the one that just said he's not supposed to talk while he's eating!"

"And he's not eating. Are you deaf? He just said he isn't hungry and a child who isn't hungry after an exam isn't normal!"

"You're making a lot of fuss over nothing! To hear you, that child's so bright he shines in the dark! It's no use asking how his exam was. His exam was fine, that's obvious, he's a genius! I can't see what you're worried about!"

She stood and picked up her empty plate and teacup.

"Me, though, I've got plenty to worry about! My lunatic got lost on his way home from school again and we won't find him till tonight — as usual! He doesn't pass his exams, oh no, he fools around and does his drawings and carries on and makes faces with a bunch of other lunatics just like him.... He doesn't go to school to learn, he plays! And he sure doesn't shine in the dark — it's hard enough to find him in the daylight! He.... He...."

She stopped. The well hadn't dried up but she couldn't find the words. Her mouth was still open, full of ugly things — accusations, complaints, curses — but nothing came out and she stood there by the sink, rooted to the spot, a tragic statue left behind in this poor kitchen, her lack of vocabulary rendering her powerless.

"Dammit all anyway.... What...what am I going to do with him? He's going to...he'll be too old to...too old for the supplementary class next September...."

It came out by fits and starts, it came out awkwardly, barely murmured and almost incomprehensible, but the fat woman's child understood that it came from unhappiness such as he'd never seen before, that was infinitely more serious, infinitely more humiliating than the stupid exam he wasn't even sure he'd actually failed. His own unhappiness seemed very small and he felt a little insulted.

Albertine summoned up the strength to rinse off her plate with cold water. She spoke to her sister-in-law without looking at her.

"We'll have him here with us all the time now...."

The fat woman gestured to her son to leave the room discreetly. He shuffled out of the kitchen feeling abandoned and betrayed.

The fat woman remained at her place, absent-mindedly playing with some breadcrumbs, trying to put on a bold front.

"Have you known for a long time?"

Albertine cleared her throat.

"I thought he'd stay another year and I'd have time to think about it.... But they phoned last week, when you were at the movies with Philippe...."

"They can't keep him any more?"

"He's too old. Him and Monique Gratton, apparently they could have a bad influence on the younger ones.... Looks like we have to find something else for him to do.... I didn't really understand...just that I'm going to have to deal with him now... They told me there's institutions for kids his age but...."

Gripping the edge of the sink, she bent over to vomit.

"I don't want to lock up my child!"

He was lying in the very middle of the chenille spread on his parents' bed. It smelled of his father a little and of his mother a lot. As he turned his head to the right he could imagine his father's long legs pulled up to his stomach, his head outside the bed as if he were getting up, a huge adult fetus the fat woman had to shake several times a night in the unlikely hope that it would make him stop snoring; on the left there was a dent his mother's body had hollowed out over the years; it made the bed slope and you wanted to roll down it like you did on the lawns in Parc Lafontaine, starting on Gabriel's side, who was too light to leave a mark in his own bed, and ending on the side of the fat woman whose mere presence carved out a place for her wherever she went; it was a toboggan slide, a ski hill, a sand dune that led to the lake, the river — to water, at any rate.

He knew his father still visited his mother's side fairly often, that he straightened out his legs and became all at once very tall, very heavy, very present in the bed; he knew because he himself still slept in the darkest corner of their bedroom, between the window and the monstrous wooden armoire, and despite their efforts to be as discreet as they could his parents sometimes let themselves go in demonstrations of pleasure that didn't lie. When he was very little he'd often thought that one of his parents, whichever one was moaning loudest, was sick and that the other was trying to help, but as he got older he understood that the sickness always caught them both at the same time, and that they gave themselves over to it with an abandon that had nothing to do with any disease: It was a game played in the dark, one that didn't include him. He had never *seen* the game because the bedroom was too dark, but he had a confused grasp of the rules that consisted of feints and attacks, of consents that had to be waited for, and abrupt, surprising refusals that took the form of questioning little sighs, and most of all, of great irrational surrenders. The odour of his parents, a single one this time, a perfect combination whose power thrilled him, rose in the room which was overheated winter and summer, and nailed him on his back, arms flung open, legs apart, offered. He waited somewhat anxiously for the cries of deliverance his parents held back as best they could, that always marked the end of their play. He shared their pleasure, though his own was not yet altogether physical; it was a relief that came from everywhere inside him and it left him drained and content. Every time, without fail, his mother would turn towards his father and whisper: "I hope we didn't wake up the little one...." His father would laugh softly, while he felt like crying out: "I'm never asleep when you do it! Never!" Often he even hoped they'd start again.

And now he was going to disappoint them both.

His heart felt squeezed, as if he had wrung it himself with his hands. He clutched the bedspread and pulled it up over his head. He saw the exam questions again, dancing before his eyes, questions he didn't understand, and his own answers that he had no memory of having written.... It was the end of every-thing: disgrace, the humiliation of failure; it was dense and black and it weighed so heavily on his chest he couldn't breathe. Nothing was possible now, his life was broken, he no longer had a future: In a few min-utes he had lost an entire year and never, ever would he make it up. Because he was too proud. Because he didn't have the courage to do it all again, to re-learn things he already knew. Because it wasn't fair. Because for a child of nine one year is the end of the world! How could he explain that in words? "I was good all year but then all of a sudden I turned dumb?" A year's punishment, repeating Grade Four, all because of one hour of uncontrollable helplessness in the face of someone else's unhappiness! He would have to answer embarrassing questions, counter humiliating accusations. He would have to struggle in a conflict that couldn't be resolved. For having been forcibly introduced into the enchanted forest whose existence he'd suspected for so long. He was annoyed at Marcel, he was annoyed at himself; something thick and slimy and depraved rose up from his solar plexus; he didn't know what it was but he knew that when it struck his brain and he could attach an image to it, he would want to die. Before it got away from him and began to destroy everything.

He was very familiar with the word "revolt," he'd come across it often in his reading, but he knew that what was germinating in him now was more perni-cious, more subtle too, and it terrified him.

He wanted to clamp his hand over his mouth to keep from crying out because his anguish was so bit-ter, but his arm touched paper, a newspaper, it must be *La Presse*. He threw off the bedspread, smoothed the crumpled paper without thinking, as if he were trying to stall for time, to put off a deadline that was inevitable but could still be manipulated a little. He realized right away just how important this page would be for his mother; suddenly his mind was cleared of all his problems, and he smiled. A new word. Television. Movies in your own house.

It was raining stars by the million. He didn't need to look at one particular corner of the sky, everywhere they were dying, leaving behind them a silent lament of golden dust. The vault, opaque and black, resembled the inside of an umbrella where all the metal ribs were luminous. Everything happened amid a slightly harrowing absence of sound: Those incandescent things falling towards him at a tremendous speed would surely create a terrible racket! He wondered if they had cut off the sound the way they did in the parish hall on Saturday afternoon when the children are too agitated and they want to punish them. But he wasn't at the movies, he wasn't even in the city, he was far, far away, deep in the Laurentians, and he was drifting on one of the million lakes up there, an ancient volcano crater ringed with evergreens that smelled intensely of pine cones.

The wharf extended some distance into the lake; he knew he was lying at the end of that long wharf and that someone, a woman, was sitting beside him, on his right, her hands on her knees, head raised towards the sky as well. The moon had not yet risen though it was very late. A distant voice, almost without intonation, one that spoke too slowly, murmured what he already knew: "There won't be any moon tonight.

The world is being punished."

He thought, It's fine with me if the world's being punished. He felt relieved, as if the moon — too present, too bright — might have jeopardized the rain of stars if she had decided to show herself.

"Why are the stars falling?" He was speaking too slowly as well. And from too far away.

The movement in the sky was so disorderly, he had to close his eyes for a moment. (In fact, the sun was warming his eyelids because one sunbeam had managed to penetrate the vault of flowers.) The voice was nearer, warmer, with finer shadings. "It's the night of the great suicide. All the stars that have had enough come pouring down on us, head over heels."

"Had enough of what?"

He opened his eyes. A face appeared, upside down, in his field of vision. First the forehead, then the eyes, and after that the rest. He had seen her die, he remembered it very well, he had watched over her soul that refused to rise into the sky. He'd been afraid of her for years and then one night during a snowstorm, he had watched as she was extinguished like an old candle when its wick has burned away. The women (Rose, Violette, Mauve, and their mother, Florence) had promised him a beautiful ceremony, with the vision of a soul leaving the body to fly away towards something lofty and substantial, but all he had seen was a fixed gaze, unbearably sad, in a face ravaged by sickness and life. Victoire. His grandmother.

"Of everything. Like you. And me."

He twisted his neck, trying to see her right side up. She placed her hand over his eyes.

"I'm not the one you should be looking at."

Through her fingers he could see quite distinctly the silent rain that would continue to fall until morning.

"Why just at night? Why do the stars only commit suicide at night, Grandma?"

The hand left his forehead and rose very high in the sky as if to gather up some stars and give them to him. A handful of burnt blueberries.

"They pick a night when there's no moon. So we can see them."

And then, with no transition, as if someone had tied a knot in time, without seeing Victoire bend over him, he felt himself being lifted up, projected towards the sky. Now they were all around him. His grandmother was holding him at arm's length, facing the dying stars. He wasn't fourteen years old now, he was every age at once, he was all the Marcel's he had ever been and all his memories formed a single memory, one that was filled with great, with tremendous sorrow. With flashes of joy that were dazzling but that were all in the past. Before him, an unbearable greyness he had no desire to know.

Someone, his grandmother, was offering him up, as he was, a sacrifice. But to whom?

An image froze in his head. A *tableau vivant* composed of four women in rocking chairs and a cat who was cleaning his muzzle with his left paw.

"You wanted to listen to them, you ate at their table, you learned their craziness, you loved them more than anybody else. You chose the road that leads to here. And that's just too bad."

She let him fall into the water. The rain of gold, tumultuous, nearly demented, continued. While his grandmother cursed the neighbour women she had always refused to see, to whom she'd always refused to bare her soul, who now were taking her grandson after they had taken away her brother — her love, her life.

At the heart of the black water, the man he had hardly known but whose spirit and stories with no beginning or end had helped him to live, was playing the violin.

The two Carmens were standing at the foot of the stairs, silent because they never had anything to say to one another when they were alone. If the whole gang was there — the fat woman's child, Jay Pee Jodoin, Linda Lauzon, Claude Lemieux, Carmen Brassard's sister Manon, Carmen Ouimet's brother, Bernard — they became voluble, talking freely, often even putting their arms around each other's waist, automatically most likely, without really thinking about it; but at the end of a day of playing, or after school when they walked home together (they were neighbours and their mothers, who didn't see much of each other, had been surprised when they'd given the same name to daughters born a few days apart), a heavy silence fell that made them uncomfortable, and they would move away from one another as if an almost palpable magnetic field were pulling them apart when they were alone.

Carmen Ouimet suffered as a result, but not Carmen Brassard.

The former, who was dull, discreet and pathologically shy, and who secretly dreamed of getting closer to her best friend even though she thought it was impossible, always let the other girl make the first move; Carmen Brassard was rebellious and often rude, but above all she was uneasy at the expectations of her friend, who she thought was too clinging, and she would fall apart, out of boredom or indifference, whenever they were alone, going out all at once like a lightbulb: One moment she was frantically kissing Jay Pee Jodoin whom she liked a little too much, or giving Claude Lemieux a friendly slap on the bum, and a moment later, when the others had gone, nothing; she would freeze in mid-gesture or break off the peal of laughter she'd been sending across Fabre Street — and go out. Carmen Ouimet would see her literally drained of energy and she blamed herself: It was her fault, she wasn't interesting enough, unlike the fat woman's child she couldn't make images appear simply by recounting things, even insignificant ones or, like Jay Pee, produce smiles that made you melt inside or even, like Claude, say silly things that made him interesting just by being silly; no, she was plain old Carmen Ouimet who had nothing to say and didn't say it.

They hadn't actually made a decision to wait for the fat woman's child at the foot of his stairs, saying something like, "We didn't see him this morning, let's sit on the steps and wait till he comes out"; no, without even exchanging a look they had crossed Fabre Street (in any case it would have been hard to explain why they almost always left their houses at the same moment, as if each girl knew that the other was also heading for the door, opening it, crossing the balcony and going down the three steps to the front yard...), then they sat there without saying a word but with similar gestures, one girl patting her hair — Carmen Brassard, proud of her auburn mane — the other smoothing the pleats of her school uniform.

A few minutes had passed. Carmen Brassard was lost in thought, humming a western song she'd heard on the radio. Carmen Ouimet was looking down at her knees. The sun had just disappeared behind the house; they were comfortable here despite the heat. For the first time, it occurred to Carmen Ouimet that speech, whether coherent conversation or small talk just to fill the time, would be superfluous and that surprised her. But she didn't have time to be happy about it: Claude Lemieux was coming out of his house across the street, yelling: "If we go to Saint-Eustache I'll run away! And you'll never find me!" They could hear his mother's voice from the very back of the house: "...do as I say, that's what you'll do! Who's the boss around here?"

In the middle of her melodic line Carmen Brassard sighed, then she shouted: "Hey, Claude, going away for the summer? Good riddance!", even though she didn't believe a word of it. He answered in the same tone: "In two days you'll miss me so much you'll have a nervous breakdown!" The upstairs door opened behind them and the fat woman's child came out on the balcony. The two Carmens stood up together. In the distance, because they lived ten houses away, they could see Carmen Ouimet's cousins Jay Pee Jodoin and Linda Lauzon running towards them. You could see their feet hit the cement and a few seconds later you could hear the sound, out of phase, unreal, as if they were running in a poorly synchronized film.

The core formed in geometrical fashion: Both Claude Lemieux and the fat woman's child had to descend a staircase to join the two Carmens, while Jay Pee and Linda were hurrying to arrive at the same time as the two boys.

They were a knot, a kernel, on Fabre Street; a knot of the intrigues of a group of children all the same age who love each other almost too much and can't help doing each other as much harm as good; the core, the source, the origin of the very life of the street: strident laughter that bursts the summer sky when no one else has the strength to play in the devastatingly scorching heat; the cries of horror during their games of hide-and-seek when the challenge was not so much to find the ones who were hiding as to scare them; the briefer but no less intense cries that rose in the icy winter air when the children jumped into snowbanks from their second floor balconies and sometimes even (Jay Pee, of course, with his stiff Pepsodent smile) from the third; the wild races to catch someone who'd just let a particularly disgusting fart; the conversations that lasted for hours and hours, on subjects as varied as their crazy teachers (brothers and nuns, the same dangerous craziness), their mothers' cooking (the specialties varied and were defended with passion), radio programmes (the fat woman's child had an obvious weakness for "Yvan l'intrépide" while Linda Lauzon swore by "Un homme et son péché" and Claude Lemieux listened lovingly every afternoon to Guy Mauffette's "Les p'tits bouts de choux"), or the latest movie shown in the parish hall, especially if by chance it had been in French.

Whenever they got together as they'd done this afternoon, without consultation but sure they would see each other, Fabre Street was ablaze with life, and other children of different ages, who occupied a rather sporadic place in their group, would envy them.

It was because they'd all been born during the same week, to mothers most of whom hadn't planned them, who made children because they were supposed to, or because sex was forbidden except with the intention of making children, and those nearly simultaneous births in the early days of the summer of 1942 welded them together in a compact block it was unthinkable to break apart. Not only were they the same age, in a sense they had the same soul, something great and powerful all six of them shared and that they were convinced — naïve youngsters that they were — they would go on sharing for the rest of their lives.

And so Claude Lemieux's imminent departure had landed in their midst like a bomb. The fat woman's child hadn't really believed him on the way home from school; thinking it was another of Madame Lemieux's threats, he'd forgotten it almost at once.

Now, Madame Lemieux could be called the queen of threats: Twenty or thirty times a day and always in language that, if it wasn't flowery was at least full of images, she would threaten her son with brutality of the worst kind, and her conviction gave goosebumps to anyone who could hear her — and they were numerous, because she talked very loud and preferably in front of an open door or window: she progressed from the house of correction (and not just any one: the one for *child criminals*, the word "criminal" being uttered with a guttural sound that made your skin crawl) to a prolonged session with the strap (not just any strap, the big, heavy, black one from which a single well-placed blow would make your bum sting for hours, and she promised him hundreds, thousands of blows, an endless series that would leave her son's backside permanently tanned); then she progressed to spending a winter night hanging from the clothesline, pinned by the ears (Claude's were big) till he turned as stiff as long underwear someone had forgotten to bring in the night before, or to imprisonment for weeks in some cupboard with the sprouting potatoes and even, when he'd done something really rotten or when she was particularly exasperated, to a session at the iron-ing-board, with Claude in the role of the pleated skirt that has to be pummelled with the iron for hours.

But when Claude came home this early afternoon he had incontrovertible proof that this time his mother wasn't exaggerating, that her threat was real and definitive: She had started packing right under his nose while he was eating.

The protests that rose up then were all the more surprising because Claude was far from the most popular member of the tribe: In a sense he was actually its scapegoat. But perhaps the children had realized that a new scapegoat would be hard to find. And that it takes a long time to train one. After all, it hadn't been very long since this one had stopped trying to fight back, and they had known him all their lives! And perhaps they also realized, vaguely, without actually saying so but feeling a tremendous pang in the sensitive region of the heart, that they really were fond of Claude Lemieux, with his banana breath and his perpetual whining. That they actually liked him quite a lot.

Linda Lauzon, the beanpole of the group, whose mother said that if she kept growing they could use her for a lightning rod on top of the cross on Mount Royal, had given him an affectionate hug though usually she pinched him at the slightest opportunity.

"When do you go?"

"I dunno.... Pretty soon I guess, 'cause my Mom started packing her dishes."

"She's doing the dishes first? That's dumb! Hasn't she ever moved before? Your dishes are the last thing you pack! What if you need them? What if you want something to eat just before you go? Or a glass of water — then what do you do?"

Carmen Brassard cut Linda off, pushing her away and taking her place next to Claude.

"What do you know about it anyway? All of a sudden you're the big packing expert but you've never moved in your life.... If you're thirsty you drink a Coke, dingbat! And if you're hungry you buy a bag of chips from Marie-Sylvia! You ought to tell your mom to move more often, we wouldn't have to put up with you all the time!"

She grabbed hold of Claude, who was grateful, because Linda Lauzon didn't smell very good. She didn't actually stink, the terrible kind of stink that makes you shiver, but the smell of dried pee on underpants that weren't washed very often wasn't pleasant. Her mother, Germaine Lauzon, was clean but Linda, who knows why, hated to change her underwear, she even hid it under her pillow so her mother couldn't find it. She'd told the two Carmens she did it out of modesty, but they didn't understand what she meant.

"Are you sure you aren't just going to your Grandma's for the summer?"

"Sure, she registered me for school out there and everything!"

There was a silence that no one broke because no one could think of any reply to this new incontrovertible argument: The school at Saint-Eustache was expecting Claude.

They'd stopped looking at each other now, perhaps for fear of breaking into sobs at the sight of their friend's undoubtedly downcast face.

The fat woman's child thought to himself that this day was cursed, a black day, though he'd thought earlier, when he'd seen the birth of summer, that he was

126

one of the privileged, the chosen, and nothing could touch him now, but here he was losing everything — his honour and his best friend.

Nor did they hear Claude Lemieux start to cry. When Carmen Ouimet looked up at him, with equal parts of jealousy and compassion because he was in Carmen Brassard's arms, the tears had already been flowing for a while down his cheeks, his nose, his quivering chin; it was the warm-up for a tantrum that was going to be violent and long and that was going to...to make them late for school! She looked at her watch (she was the only member of the group who had one and it was used for outings when they had to be home at a precise time, like the movies or a walk in Parc Lafontaine), and let out a piercing cry that brought back to life the group frozen in stupor.

"Holy cow, it's three minutes to one! We're going to be late!"

The flight of a bird scared by a rifle shot or the intrusion of a predator. Without thinking about it — not even Claude Lemieux who could hardly see where he was going because he was blinded by tears — all six started running as fast as they could; they had crossed the lane, they were almost at Gilford Street. Six birds wild with fright were racing to their schools, Saint-Stanislas and Saints-Anges, the boys turning the corner at Gilford, the girls continuing along the girls' road. No goodbyes, no see you laters, no good luck in your exams, they could only think about getting there before the bell rang.

As he passed 1474 Gilford, the fat woman's child felt nothing; he thought to himself, *Marcel's not there now, the enchanted forest is deserted and life's not worth living any more.*

He had witnessed the whole scene, making himself as small as he could underneath the outside staircase. He was thirteen years old and they were nine, yet he was the one who was hiding, quaking with fear at the thought of being discovered, concealed here behind a scrawny bush whose nondescript foliage was etiolated for lack of sun, his heart stopping whenever one of the children turned to look his way, thrilled to hear that Claude Lemieux was moving (one less!) but torn apart by the pain he could see on his cousin's face.

After all, if he should announce out of the blue that he was leaving, that he was going to disappear, maybe forever, would anyone, anyone at all for God's sake, be upset like that? Wouldn't he instead see relief on their faces, behind the token protests? The signs were unmistakable: his mother's eyes that lit up in spite of herself when something good happened so suddenly she didn't have time to assume the proper expression; his aunt's lower lip that she wrinkled when she didn't want anyone to know how happy she was — generally because of some clever move by her son; his cousin who suddenly turned red because of some explosion of happiness.... Is that what he'd see on his family's faces, rather than normal sorrow, unbearable pain, if he, Marcel, were to go away —

Marcel, whom they were *supposed* to love, yes, it was a duty, they were *supposed* to love him because he was the most unfortunate of them all?

Duplessis had been shamelessly abandoning him for some time now, but if he told his cat that now *he* was abandoning *him*, that he was leaving for...that he was going to a country where there's no place for cats, even miraculous ones, even magical ones, what would happen? Would Duplessis reappear all at once, fat, silky, happy, glorious, to tell him it was just a trick, I only did it to tease you, come here and we'll cuddle for three whole days. Or would he cry out, rolling his r's the way he did when he wanted to make fun of Marcel, Good r-r-r-riddance, the devil's leaving us?

He tried to imagine Fabre Street without him: It was easy; he didn't see the slightest difference. He sank a little deeper into his black melancholy because he realized immediately that Fabre Street would indeed go on without him, unchanged by his departure, it might even be relieved not to see the little runt hanging around with his hopeless despair, his lies that weren't lies, his loves that he didn't know how to express, that emerged from him as waves of aggressiveness towards everyone he'd have liked to overwhelm with affection. He was a negligible quantity on Fabre Street, an adolescent with a shameful disease that offended his family, an idiot who could do nothing except scribble drawings to order because he couldn't learn anything else.... No, that wasn't true.... He turned his head towards the yard next door, the wooden steps up to the front stoop, the varnished door that always shone a little brighter than the doors on Fabre Street.... It contained everything that was known in the world, all the happiness, the grace, the indescribable grace of knowledge. And it was getting away from him layer by layer, he was being stripped, undressed of all that and he didn't deserve it. He didn't deserve it!

He wished he could cry out, a good loud cry of revolt that would stupefy the whole street as it was contemplating the first hours of summer, but he heard a sound overhead and hunched his head into his shoulders again. It was the sound of very familiar footsteps. The tap, tap of stiletto heels on the balcony, on the top steps. His mother was coming down the stairs.

He hadn't seen the children run away, didn't know how long he'd been "lost" in his imagination. It could be just one o'clock or a quarter to four: These absences, very different from his fits, varied in length, but always seemed amazingly brief.

He saw his mother's legs, the edge of her skirt, her waist, her neck. "She's looking for me! She's going to yell my name in the middle of the street and I'll be ashamed, again! And then she'll look under the stairs!" He huddled a little deeper inside the scrawny bush and he was positive he'd made a terrible noise.

Albertine stopped at the foot of the stairs, straightened the nylons she wore so rarely, that had a tendency to droop.

This was the first time he had seen her from the back when she thought she was alone. And she seemed surprisingly vulnerable in her blue and white polka-dot dress. He stuck his head outside the bush, wrinkling his nose and forehead. The steps divided her into four distinct parts: head and shoulders, back, rear end, legs. She seemed to hesitate between continuing on her way towards Mont-Royal or going back up the stairs. She pushed the handle of her purse towards her elbow, smoothed her hair which was frizzy at the nape of her neck, coughed into her fist uncomfortably, then resumed walking at a good clip as if she'd just made the most important decision of her life.

When she was outside the L'Heureux house, he came out of his hiding place, positioned himself in the middle of the sidewalk, and looked at her even more closely. A good part of his own troubles, all dressed up and looking almost stylish, was walking towards Mont-Royal, unaware that he was watching her, exquisitely fragile. Seen from this angle she was all in all an insignificant woman...no, not insignificant — harmless: a full skirt swaying from side to side, a twitch in the right elbow because the purse kept getting in her way, her feet, unaccustomed to high heels, hesitating at the cracks in the sidewalk.... No outburst, no screaming, no threats, not even a hint of anything of the sort.... A woman like his aunt, but not so fat. And that's all! She didn't respond to a greeting from Madame Jodoin who was sweeping her bit of sidewalk, but she wasn't hostile either.

He tilted his head onto his left shoulder and thought, *You should always look at your troubles from behind.*

The bell rang just as the three boys stepped inside the schoolyard, so there was no time to wish each other good luck in the geography exam. Jay Pee Jodoin joined the ranks of Grade Four B, while the fat woman's child and Claude Lemieux took their usual places with their classmates.

The atmosphere at Saint-Stanislas had changed since morning. The really big one, the most feared, the most hated, the horrible French exam, was over; it had been hard, as hard for the Grade Nines as for the Grade Fours, there'd been a lot of talk about it, they had insulted, defiled and cursed the mysterious French language experts somewhere in Quebec City who had concocted it, the children had wished them a terrible summer accompanied by every kind of suffering and disease, each one more venereal and fatal than the rest; but the one this afternoon would be easier because they weren't really afraid of Geography or Math. Sure, a few dumbbells who couldn't remember the capitals of Manitoba and Ontario, or who shuddered at the sight of the division sign, might be anxious, but they were a minority of real dunces, the ones who spent part of the school year in the corner, noses to the wall, or at the door of the Vice Principal's office, waiting to be strapped. Or hopeless cases like

Claude Lemieux, who were tolerated in the normal classes in spite of everything because the supplementary class was already full.

And so there was a certain nonchalance in the behaviour of the Saint-Stanislas pupils who that morning had been quaking with fear: It took many forms, from picking their noses to telling dirty jokes behind the back of the person ahead of you to make him laugh, to loud, ostentatious yawns and the inevitable smirks and upthrust middle fingers exchanged between classes to prove their virility.

The fat woman's child, though, was worried sick. He kept watching Frère Robert, fearing the moment when the teacher would give him a curious or uncomprehending look, the kind that meant: "What got into you this morning, for heaven's sake?" or: "Did you do it on purpose to shame us — you, one of our best students?" but he knew perfectly well that their exams weren't marked at school but would be shipped at the end of the day to another one, where a teacher who didn't know him was going to laugh at him or read his moronic answers with a total indifference that was even more insulting. Another ignoramus: Zero. He'll just have to repeat Grade Four.

Repeat Grade Four! He saw himself with a bunch of morons younger than him who would hate him because, of course, he'd know everything before the teacher (the same one?) even opened his mouth. A whole year of anxiety and disgrace, watching his friends who, even though they weren't as good as he was, would learn things still forbidden to him because while he was usually so controlled, he had let himself be distracted, disturbed by some moron's idiotic behaviour!

Something that resembled not true hatred, because the fat woman's child was absolutely incapable of hating his cousin, but a kind of resentment towards Marcel, sprang up somewhere in the region of his heart. Not in his head, it wasn't anything rational; it felt hot and it twisted in his chest, formed a knot in his throat and climbed no higher. It was also different from the revolt he'd felt in his parents' bedroom an hour earlier, because it was directed outside rather than towards himself. And it happened very fast, while his class was starting to move. He set one foot in front of the other, felt something like a slight shudder, and then the tiny inner explosion occurred, out of nowhere and absolutely uncontrollable, it climbed up his spine, stopped in his throat like a suggestion of a little mouse's cry that no one, fortunately, could hear. Then he felt an urge to beat up on his cousin that departed in the same quick breath: He wanted to tear him limb from limb, slice off his head; it was violent, urgent, vital; and then he only wanted to forget him, to cover him with the condescending contempt he deserved, because really he didn't deserve anything else. All that came and went in rapid waves and he felt torn between contradictory feelings that made him dizzy. At first he'd been ashamed of himself in the face of a new weakness; now he was experiencing a new-found urge to destroy someone else, that he hadn't even suspected when he woke up that morning. In any case, he was walking behind the other pupils, automatically, not thinking of what he was doing. He was heading for his classroom where perhaps another failure lay in wait that would give him an even stronger urge to murder his cousin. Though it was innocent, as he knew perfectly well.

He walked past Frère Robert with his head lowered. He even shrank back a little, surprising his
teacher, as if he was expecting a clip on the head. It
was the behaviour of a class dummy, of a moron used
to being caught and to paying for every single trick
from the lowest to the most insignificant, it was a
reflex so unlike him that Frère Robert, who already
had found his behaviour that morning very strange,
decided to watch him more closely. This child, usually
calm and quite brilliant, had come to class late and
covered with mud, at the same time and in the same
condition as his cousin, the lunatic, who was perhaps
starting to have a bad influence on him; he'd been
impolite and one of the last to turn in his exam
though he usually finished with surprising speed.
Since this morning everything about him had been
astonishing.

Frère Robert had seen brilliant pupils crack up
during exams before, for no apparent reason; they
would sit at their desks as if everything was normal,
then collapse over an exam that wasn't necessarily a
hard one, and they wouldn't recover. Was it threats by
overly strict parents that laid them low, or their own
nervous systems snapping? When questioned they usually said they didn't know what had happened, didn't
understand, they were sure that if they had to write
the same exam again they'd sail through it, that it had
been like a hole, a void, a fleeting blank they could
not control.... Occasionally he sensed that it was hiding something deeper, more serious, but he was rarely
able to make them speak.

Frère Robert had no way of knowing if it was
happening to this pupil: All the copies of that morning's examination were already in the principal's office,

probably sealed inside ridiculous "secret" or "confidential" envelopes that were absolutely inviolable — even if a nine-year-old boy's future depended on it.

He would keep a close eye on him then during the two exams that afternoon, even if it meant cheating during recess by sneaking a look at his geography exam. He had read the questions before going down to the schoolyard and thought they were particularly childish. But if his pupil showed signs of any trouble with this exam, would he dare to intervene?

The fat woman's child looked up just before he climbed the few steps to the door of the school. Peter Pan? Yes, Peter Pan was there, on the roof of the school, leaning over the gutter, smiling at the fat woman's child as he looked at him. The schoolyard, a big cement square now nearly empty, shone in the sun with a very white light that made him blink. He could come down to the fat woman's child, throw himself at him, become him, pull him up above, hold him out and swing him right there in the sky to make him laugh, or he could let the child come to him, give him the freedom to join him on the roof, let himself be surrounded, then hurl himself into space with him, not altogether sure who was who or which one was leading the other. Anyway, it would be a relief. Very briefly. As usual. But then the fat woman's child looked down and the contact was broken. Any urge to somersault in the sun was gone now and he resigned himself to following the others.

The thirty-one pupils in Grade Four C took their seats amid a seething of ill-contained murmurs and nervous laughter: Merely walking through the door into the classroom had revived this morning's demons. The exam questions were piled on the teacher's desk and all eyes turned to them.

136

It didn't matter that Geography was easier than French: A bad mark, especially at the end of the year, was disastrous. They all started mentally reciting the capitals of Canada's ten provinces: that had been the year's big item, along with the natural resources of each province, its area, and — worst of all, and what a horror it was! — where they were *located* in the country. Foreheads were furrowed, brows were knit, tight.... Jigsaw puzzles depicting Canada took shape, were deformed, assumed comic appearances verging on the ridiculous. All right, what was that fish-shaped province right next to Quebec? And the three flat ones where nothing grows but Corn Flakes? How about the one at the other end of the world with those unreal-looking mountains? Pretty Columbia? The faces of those who knew the answer lit up briefly like that of a saint in mid-miracle, the others lowered their heads and wished their desks contained the geography books they'd hated so much all year.

The fat woman's child was watching Frère Robert's every move, which seemed to be very slow. He wished everything would happen quickly, wanted the exam questions on his desk right now, wanted to read them, understand them or not, wanted to know, finally, if his brain had really been turned into white sauce during the night, or if this morning's adventure had been just a passing weakness.

Frère Robert slowly picked up the pile of exam questions, knocked it against his desk, seemed to estimate its weight *(He's so slow...just hand them out or else I will...why does he have to play with our nerves like that...)*, descended the step from the platform, walked up to the first desk in the first row....

The fat woman's child turned his head towards Claude Lemieux to stave off his impatience. A vision

137

of horror. Claude Lemieux hadn't the faintest idea what Geography might be, or a country or a capital; he always stared at a map as if it were a particularly menacing drawing, and so incomprehensible he could stare at it, motionless, for minutes at a time without realizing the teacher was talking to him. He was hypnotized by the absurdity of Geography. Now he looked so white it was frightening, and slumped so low it was as if he wanted to disappear into the floor.

Frère Robert was speaking. The fat woman's child jumped.

"You'll like this one. It's at your level. It's just about the province of Quebec. Even Lemieux has a chance with this one."

A great sigh of relief. A few "hurrays," weak ones.

Guy Thivierge, who sat in the first desk in the third row where the fat woman's child also sat, was approaching — also too slowly. He winked at his friend François Wilhelmy with whom he was going to try to cheat by any means possible, which weren't many given the location of their respective desks.

Finally, the sheet of paper was set down in front of him. He closed his eyes, offered a short prayer of the kind in which you promise God you'll behave yourself for the rest of your days if He grants what you want, took a deep breath....

It was consummately idiotic.

Instead of relief at recovering his wits, he was overwhelmed by a flash of rage. This time it didn't come from his solar plexus or his heart: It was carefully thought-out, cold and surprisingly controlled — and exceptionally ugly.

A few brief minutes took care of the exam: capital city, natural resources, approximate area, name of

Prime Minister (a question that would come back in the Canadian History exam next Monday), the rivers, their tributaries, etc. He wrote in great bursts as if each question were a personal insult, without thinking because it was too much trouble to re-read his answers, he just raced — he was the first one to finish, of course — to leave his paper on the desk of Frère Robert, who was flabbergasted.

The fat woman's child was back in the empty schoolyard, where he sat on one of the cement steps. He was panting. Peter Pan wasn't there because he had absolutely no need of him now.

All of this was Marcel's fault, after all. And Marcel was going to pay. Dearly.

Had his aunt not called him he wouldn't have gone home that afternoon. As usual, though it was getting harder and harder, he'd have tried to find sanctuary with Florence and her daughters. But his aunt was there on the balcony, tangible and real, she was calling softly to him as she leaned on the railing, her huge breasts resting on her folded arms. It was possible she'd been looking out for him for quite a while.

"Marcel, come in and eat. You must be hungry, it's past one-thirty...."

Once again he had lost all notion of time. He had watched his mother walk away in the direction of Mont-Royal and after she was out of sight he had gone on looking in the same direction, standing in the middle of the sidewalk, leaning forward slightly, as tense and feverish as if he were waiting for the signal to start a mysterious race in which he was the only competitor, a very important race that would take him to a place he'd never dared go to, a new destination he had just discovered and desperately needed to reach. Minutes had passed without his realizing it. If his aunt hadn't yanked him from his dream, would he have stood there all afternoon, like a statue on a bedroom dresser?

He didn't move right away, torn between wanting to run, to take refuge in the neighbours' house, and his gurgling stomach he'd just become aware of, thanks to his aunt's interruption.

"Make up your mind, Marcel, I'm not waiting all afternoon! I have other things to do!"

He made up his mind. But by becoming someone who needs coaxing, who complies with another's wishes just to make them happy, because honestly as far as he's concerned.... He trudged up the stairs, stopped halfway to pick at a scab of paint, lingered again at the turn in the stairs to tie a shoelace that wasn't undone. His aunt watched, hiding a grin he would have been insulted to see. He wanted to make her lose patience like his mother, but he only managed to amuse her.

When he came up to his aunt, he yawned.

She straightened up, turned and went inside.

"Being a teenager's no fun, is it? Nothing's fun, everybody gets on your nerves, life's not worth living.... But meanwhile they can hear your stomach growling all the way to Gilford Street."

He made a face behind her back.

"And keep your faces for your mother. I don't have to do what I'm doing, so don't bug me! Just wash your hands and sit down and eat! If you aren't at the table in two minutes flat, you'll have to wait till supper!"

Her harsh tone was phony, he knew that perfectly well. With an impatient sigh, he headed for the bathroom. If only she had really attacked him, he would have answered back, they'd have fought, and it would have felt so good; but no, he knew he could keep her waiting as long as he wanted, his meal would still be there when he came out of the bathroom and that was discouraging.

When he was little he'd been very fond of his aunt. From a distance though, because she already had three sons whom she hovered over lovingly, and he'd always been afraid she would push him away if he got too near. And so he stayed close to his own mother, who was dry and mean and didn't surround him and Thérèse with love at all; who often frightened him with her unpredictable mood swings; whom he'd have been glad to trade for anyone else's mother, especially her — the mother of his cousins, the perfect mother, who had plenty of cuddles and soothing words and smiles that turned your heart upside down. But for a while now his aunt's very kindness, her affection, her understanding, her angelic patience, the scent of Chénard's "Tulipe Noire" she gave off the minute spring arrived, her vast dresses of worn-out, flowered cotton softened from washing, in short everything about her that he used to love so much, now only got on his nerves. As if he no longer believed in her. Because when you get right down to it, nobody could be that good.

As Duplessis disappeared, as he lost contact with Rose, Violette, Mauve, and their mother, he'd started to doubt everything. Especially anything good. And his aunt had always been among the best.

He remembered very clearly when it all began.

Duplessis had developed his first holes and for days he hadn't been treating Marcel very nicely. And his music lesson with Violette that afternoon had been a disaster. He had come home furious and behaved obnoxiously with his mother and his aunt. His mother had left the mark of her hand where it hurts worst, making his cheek puff up before your eyes. His aunt had taken him aside and tried to make him tell her what was wrong. And for the first time she had annoyed him. What business was it of hers? Why did she always have to know everything? So she could make fun of him again, so she could tell her children and her husband (who was just as nice and just as dull as she was) he'd become unbearable and that she felt sorry for poor Albertine for having given birth to such a monster? He told her quite simply that he had problems, yes, big ones, but they were his business and nobody else's and she'd be better off keeping an eye on her youngest, who spied on everybody in the house, who was always somewhere he shouldn't be or had his ear plastered against a door behind which things were being said that didn't concern him, instead of nagging him with her nosy questions.

She had frowned and for the first time commented on his budding adolescence. Marcel, who didn't feel in the least like an adolescent, in fact didn't even know what it meant, thought she was just being dumb. Before leaving him, she promised not to ask him any more questions, but reminded him she was always there, if he ever wanted to talk she'd always listen — and that made him even more angry.

Since then they hadn't really talked again, but every move she made, every one of those stupid little smiles, whether knowing or strictly benevolent, every one of her pleasant remarks about every inhabitant of the house, got on his nerves. He was surprised to find himself following her around the house to catch any flaw in her goodness. In the end, he placed her next to his mother on his altar of contempt.

With his hands reeking of lavender because he hadn't dried them properly, he came back to the kitchen where in fact a meal was waiting for him.

There was a horrible smell of eggs in white sauce in the house and he couldn't wait, though he was famished, to push away his plate and tell her how it made him sick. But to his amazement he saw a delicious-looking cheese-and-tomato sandwich with lettuce and mayonnaise, his favourite. He wished he had the courage to refuse it but he was salivating and had to put his hand over his mouth. Happy and sure she'd pleased him, the fat woman leaned against the stove and smiled.

Furious at her for being so nice and at himself for being such a coward, he sat at the table and began to wolf his sandwich, slurping and smacking his lips because he knew she hated that.

Something he did, or maybe it was the look he shot at her while he was chewing his first mouthful roused his aunt's curiosity and she froze briefly while she was pouring him a glass of milk. She set the bottle on the table, sat down across from him, and watched closely while he ate. He felt like telling her to screw off but he was so hungry he gobbled his lunch as if he hadn't eaten for a week.

After finishing the first half of his sandwich, he downed half of his milk. And it was then, as he was wiping away his white mustache with his shirt-sleeve, that she spoke.

"You're eating like you do after one of your spells. Were you sick this morning?"

He went on as if he hadn't heard, but from the way he slowed down for the second half of his sandwich she knew she had guessed right.

"Don't you want to talk about it?"

He turned his head while he chewed, looked at the stove, the icebox, like someone feeling lonely in a room where there was no one else.

His aunt leaned across the table towards him.

"Marcel, don't act as if I'm not there! As big as I am, I'd be hard to miss!"

He looked at her, still slurping.

"Yeah, I can see you. So what?"

"Don't pretend you didn't hear what I asked you.... And quit making those noises when you eat!"

He swallowed, ran his tongue across his teeth, slowly chewed a piece of tomato that had fallen out of the sandwich, belched with obvious satisfaction.

"That was good. Thanks a lot."

To keep from jumping on him she got to her feet, collected his plate and glass, and set them in the sink.

He hadn't budged.

With her back to him, she turned on the tap to rinse the dishes.

"And don't act so independent, I know you want to talk about it. Otherwise you'd have gone to your room long before this...."

Marcel's chair was tipped back, the fat woman heard racing footsteps, and then the bathroom door slammed.

"If anybody wants me I'm in the shithouse!"

She stood for a few moments without moving, then she resumed doing what she'd done every day for more than twenty years: put the kettle on to boil, separated the cups and glasses from the plates, sprinkled some dish soap into the plastic dishpan (plastic was the one new thing that had come into the kitchen over the past three years: because everybody was talking about it, it was apparently the material of the future — Gabriel had bought some blue plastic glasses that tasted of blue plastic, red plastic plates that got scratched right away and that she wished she could throw in the garbage, and a green plastic dishpan that got soft when the water was too hot), waited at the stove, swaying slowly till the water came to a boil....

She was fifty-one now, the age when her sisters had long since been grandmothers, the age when most women had already raised their families and now found themselves alone with their husbands, and bored. It's true she had no time to get bored in this house that was always full of noise and activity and endless squabbles and reconciliations that were ever more tumultuous, but a tremendous dissatisfaction had been insinuating itself inside her for a while now. It seemed as if her two older sons didn't want to leave home, to say nothing of getting married, though they both had good jobs and could have rented an apartment, cut once and for all the umbilical cord that tied them to her too closely, start a family, have children; as for the youngest whom she'd had, whom she'd wanted when she was past forty and for whom she felt an irrational love, the way you love a grandchild in fact, his tremendous fragility worried her: Had she given birth to a feeble child because she no longer had the strength she'd had at twenty or thirty to raise him, bring him up, nudge him into life? She would be sixty years old when he was twenty and the thought depressed her. If Richard and Philippe persisted in not marrying, would she have to wait till she was an old woman to know her grandchildren? She saw herself spending the rest of her life washing red and blue plastic dishes for her children as they grew older and older, more and more dependent on her because never in a million years would they do a lick of housework, and she wanted to break everything. But the plastic dishes were unbreakable; apparently that was one of their great virtues.

The water started whistling in the kettle.

A lump came to her throat and the helpless feeling that overwhelmed her more and more often crept into her somewhere around her heart. She put her hand on her forehead.

"Is that all I've lived for?"

Then she heard the sound of sobbing from the bathroom and remembered that someone in this house, an adolescent who was insane, an unwanted child, a boy condemned to solitude, was living a tragedy far more horrible than hers.

He wasn't supposed to leave the schoolyard but he was very tempted. He was leaning against the fence, looking at the profile of Saint-Stanislas on the other side of de Lanaudière. Behind the church was Gilford Street and on Gilford Street....

He had found a way to punish Marcel. It would just take a few minutes, it would be violent and therefore a relief, and he was sure Marcel would never plague him again. But it would be his first act of violence and he hesitated. First he'd thought of covering his cousin with insults, creating a scene of relentless brutality, but he knew that when he wanted to be, Marcel was impervious to whatever was being said around him, so why waste his spit, struggle to find the right word, the supreme insult, if the person it was aimed at just gave him a blank stare and a condescending smirk? No, words weren't enough, he had to do something, something definitive that would permanently cut the ties that had always joined them, because he wanted to break off all contact with Marcel. He wished he could erase him from his memory, look through him as if he didn't exist, walk around him when they met, wished he were free, finally, to walk down the street by himself without sensing the presence of his goddamn cousin behind him — that insignificant slug, that tagalong who followed him like a shadow because he couldn't think for himself and had no independence. Everything was mixed up in his head, the words that came to him didn't always go together, what they added up to was at the same time vague and very clear: vague because he had trouble articulating his thoughts, but clear because the ultimate destruction of Marcel stood out very precisely.

He was still alone in the schoolyard. He had ten or fifteen minutes before the others started coming out in boisterous groups. Because the other Saint-Stanislas pupils, with nothing to think about but their little exam, would take the time to re-read their answers, correct their mistakes, form their letters very carefully, while in his case, after this morning's failure hadn't he just put down whatever came into his mind so he could leave the classroom as soon as possible to...to satisfy that thirst for revenge he was feeling for the first time in his life? A final geography exam isn't something you polish off in ten minutes, even if it's easy! And what if it hadn't been easy, if he'd just pretended it was so he could be done with it, what if he'd made a fool of himself yet again because of his goddamn cousin! What about that? An urge to run, to cross de Lanaudière, sprint across the yard behind the church by jumping over the little metal railings, was so strong he had to grip the fence with both hands. He took a quick look at the roof of the school. Still no sign of Peter Pan.

But no witnesses either!

The rest happened all by itself.

He really had the impression that his brain hadn't wanted him to, had even forbidden him to do it, but for the third time that day he *saw himself* doing it, as if he were a spectator; the asphalt that already felt warm even though summer had just begun, the cement sidewalk, the grass of the lawn, all sped by beneath his feet as in a film with the camera at ground level. He told himself that if he were an animal, a cat or dog, he would see the world from that perspective. Sounds had diminished too; all he could hear was his own heart, which was definitely beating too fast, and the air rushing out of his lungs. Usually he could control his daydreams, he chose them, grabbed them, gave them whatever form, colour, odour he wanted; he had invented Peter Pan, in fact, after reading the book by Monsieur Sir James Barrie, to give his fantasies a shape, to experience them through someone who could fly, in other words to permit himself everything; but it wasn't Peter Pan who was racing towards Gilford Street, Peter Pan would have flown, while this new body he'd settled into was racing, leaping like a little animal, that little striped animal, foul-mouthed but beautiful as sin, whose lair he was going to destroy forever....

He knew the enchanted forest was empty because he hadn't felt anything when he'd passed it a few minutes earlier. Marcel must have finished his sweet dreams and gone back home satisfied, lucky him, overwhelmed with images so splendid they would nourish him for a long time. Was all of that, the wild race, the urge to destroy, dictated by mere jealousy? He put the thought aside because he didn't want to face it right now, and walked up to the bleeding hearts.

But it was ridiculous to begin his work of destruction like that, from the outside; someone might see him, the old woman who lived at 1474 could come out with her broom and chase him away, calling him terrible names. The police could come and arrest him, throw him in jail.... And where would he put the branches he'd have ripped off the plants? No, what was needed was not an explosion but an implosion.

Marcel's cathedral had to collapse on itself so he would find it in a pitiful little heap rather than scattered all over the sidewalk and the street.

He was himself again, not Peter Pan or a tiger-striped cat, just a poor little boy sick with jealousy of a cousin who was different from the other children, and sick with worry as he contemplated his first felony. He was perfectly aware of it, and perfectly ashamed of what he was going to do, but he felt he had to. To regain a certain peace, even if he would pay later with a fleeting sense of guilt — or so he tried to convince himself.

He gently pushed the gate and now its creaking sounded absolutely charming, though just that morning it had made him shudder. Nobody on the balcony. The old lady must be taking a nap or sitting by her radio, knitting. But a rocking chair had been there since this morning, proof that the old lady really did exist and could come out and rock there whenever she wanted. He'd have to move fast. He bent down. No one in the enchanted forest either, but he knew that already. He crouched down and crawled on his hands and knees.

He felt like a key that was being inserted in a magic lock. For a few seconds he didn't move and then he rolled over, exactly like a key turning in a lock. But nothing happened. This wasn't the ritual that released the unbearable beauty he had imagined was inside Marcel's head, in Marcel's dream that had climbed up his own arm before it exploded in his brain. No, the darkness was still there. The dampness too.

He lay on his back to gaze at the bleeding hearts one last time before he murdered them.

He tried to imagine Marcel in the same position, patiently waiting for the enchantment to break over him. Could he hear the waves coming or did they catch him by surprise just when he was beginning to think that nothing was going to happen on that day, after a long moment of feverish expectation? Was it Marcel who provoked them or did they simply turn up like runaway horses to take hold of his soul? And how did he feel when he emerged from it? Overcome with happiness? Exhausted from all the sensations and smells? Did he come away with a treasure buried in his brain from which he could take whatever he wanted, for as long as he wanted?

Lucky Marcel!

And what about him? If he didn't destroy it, would this yard remain just a square of stinking earth fouled by generations of cats, circled with rust and surmounted by a grove of humble pink flowers, was there some way to grab hold of all that, to...to steal it, yes, yes, that was the right word, he wanted to rob Marcel, to pilfer his dreams, burglarize them once and for all, to see what it was like to be a...

He sat up abruptly. His forehead was in the flowers. A bleeding heart tickled his nose, making him squint. He got rid of it by squeezing it in his fist, like a fly.

...to see what it was like to be one of the chosen!

He pulled his knees up towards his face. His mouth located the scab from this morning which was coming loose and tasted again of freshly dried blood.

One of the chosen! Marcel was one of the chosen, and he wasn't. He moved his tongue from the little scab and his forehead touched down between his knees. And he saw the futility of his quest, of his enterprise of destruction, he saw the irrelevance of his own pretensions too; he sensed more than he understood the universe that separated him and Marcel; for the first time he caught a glimpse of his own inadequacy, because he had not been summoned, and it would be his fate merely to observe, to be a spectator, as he had already been a spectator of himself three times since this morning, observing as a spectator the...the genius of another person.

The genius!

Why bother to destroy the enchanted forest if the enchanted forest existed inside Marcel?

His rage was so great, his jealousy so bitter, he thought he was going to die right then and there; such pain was unbearable and you could only die of it, your fist raised to heaven while blasphemy of unheard-of violence poured from you. If he had really known any blasphemies, genuine ones, the kind that insult the gods and make them leap from their thrones deep inside their seventh heaven or the final cavern of their hell, he would have stood up in the middle of the bushes, extended his arm, clenched his fist and howled hard enough to tear his throat a rosary, a novena, of those succulent and liberating words that relieve the soul for a brief moment while smearing those who'd had the bad taste to create us.

But the only words that occurred to him were the pitiful gurglings, the insignificant by-products of blasphemy, the ridiculous derivatives of insults he was used to hearing his father, his uncles and, more recently, his brothers come out with when they'd been drinking or lacked the proper vocabulary. But those words were clearly inadequate for expressing the magnitude, the intensity of his pain. His mind was utterly devoid of words, yet it overflowed with horrible things that crawled in the dark, that would have liked to take flight, to wipe out the entire universe.

Then a thought came to him like a little glimmer in the dark, something you can cling to so as not to die. Maybe there was some way to plunder Marcel without taking his place. He just had to listen to his cousin, even make him talk, incite his confidence, and record it all in his head...and afterwards use it. All he had to do was sign the dreams of someone else so that people would think they were his. Even that he'd invented them. Perhaps, finally, he had been put on earth to be a spectator. It was a pitiful destiny, yes, but it was his own glimmer of light deep in his own darkness and he held out his arms to it.

The key was withdrawn from the magic lock where nothing marvellous at all had happened and the fat woman's child found himself with no transition on the road to school where another troublesome exam awaited.

She had stopped in front of the window cluttered with dry goods that were yellow from months, perhaps years in the sun, she had pushed back a lock of hair in a gesture devoid of coquetry, a precise, dry, automatic gesture by a woman whose hair must be not necessarily beautiful, but *in place*. She had made sure her patent-leather purse was shut, her shoes polished, her hem straight.

She guessed rather than saw her own silhouette in the big window behind which rolls of fabric, packages of rickrack braid, dozens of zippers bound together with old dried-up elastics, trimmings brown with dust, and ribbons whose colour had long since departed, had been tossed every which way.

She thought the window looked a little like St. Lawrence Boulevard and she'd said so to Mr. Schiller, who had merely smiled as he said with his inimitable accent: "To do my window every month I'm not interested. To waste time I don't want — all what I want is to make money."

She had the impression Mr. Schiller was barricading himself behind his messy window: You couldn't see inside the store when you were on the street and you couldn't tell what the weather was like when you were inside. But to her, oddly enough, that sense of confinement, that smell of never-aired cloth and dust — the same one that had been drifting there forever — was not unpleasant. At home, unless everything smelled of floor wax, lemon oil, and Spic and Span, she was sure she was living in grime and she'd succumb to depression brought on by guilt. But here, under the yellowish light, in this obvious slovenliness where there wasn't enough air and where winter and summer the atmosphere was filled with dry heat that caught at your throat, she felt as if she were in a cocoon, protected from everything, hidden from the rest of the world, and she could spend hours rummaging through old boxes of buttons or broken barrettes. Mr. Schiller or his assistant, the dreadful Mademoiselle Robitaille, an impressive walking inventory who sported the beginnings of a mustache that made her look like a seal, sometimes found her on hands and knees, her nose in a box of old patterns from the thirties and forties, claiming she was looking for a style, but obviously having an attack of voluntary amnesia. Mr. Schiller's store cost less than the movies and it worked just as well.

Obviously there was another reason for Albertine's frequent visits to Schiller's dry goods store, one that was much deeper and infinitely harder to admit: Mr. Schiller himself.

You couldn't say she was actually interested in him, Albertine having long since been beyond such considerations, but his courtesy, even though tinged with an obvious interest in making the smallest sale, disturbed her and thrilled her. It was so long since anyone had shown her any courtesy, she was glad to let herself sink into Mr. Schiller's compliments; her suspicion of all human beings, acquired by dint of crude, unsubtle suffering, came apart in his presence and she found herself defenseless. Besides, he wasn't a foul-mouthed French Canadian who can't express himself or a goddamn Frenchman with his flowery words; she liked his grating, singsong accent, the way he used her language but more subtly, with different constructions: his compliments weren't sickly-sweet or fancy; they were blunt and, when you got right down to it, it was their very abruptness that resembled him, and that was what she liked.

She came to Mr. Schiller's store in search of the little bit of human warmth she had long since refused from anybody else, even her own children.

She was about to push open the door when a tableau whose significance she didn't grasp right away made her freeze. Its three subjects were in profile: Madame Jodoin was buying buttons or something else very small that she was looking for in a box on the counter, Mr. Schiller was waiting on her with his usual smile, and Mademoiselle Robitaille was observing them. Albertine pressed her nose against the glass door, her hand shielding her eyes to get a better look at them. Something in this tableau, she couldn't say exactly what, was making her extremely uncomfortable. She tilted her head a little towards her right shoulder. A kind of false innocence emanated from those three individuals — that was it, something that claimed to be innocent but wasn't. Mademoiselle Robitaille was less relaxed than she wanted to appear, Madame Jodoin was preoccupied with something besides looking for her buttons, and Mr. Schiller — Mr. Schiller was treating her with courtesy!

Albertine straightened up. She had just seen herself in the same position as Gabrielle Jodoin, *pretending* to be looking for something, while with his charming accent Mr. Schiller paid her a barely-disguised compliment. Mr. Schiller gave her neighbour and probably all his customers, the same treatment he gave her! He brought out his courtesy not to be pleasant but to sell buttons. She wasn't jealous of Gabrielle Jodoin, but an old sense of fatalism — *I knew it couldn't last, it had to be hiding something* — suddenly surfaced. She considered herself ridiculous and naïve, she was ashamed as she saw herself again, a silly fool on her hands and knees on the dirty floorboards, all at once she understood Mademoiselle Robitaille's sickly smiles, she saw herself with all the other foolish women from the Plateau Mont-Royal lined up outside the drygoods store in the hope of picking up some measly compliment that would give her the courage to pursue a little longer her...her calvary, yes, her calvary, her life was a calvary! She'd forgotten for a few minutes, but life was a calvary! Her rage was so powerful, so searing, she had to lean against the door, causing it to open slightly and setting off the electric bell that always startled her when she was inside the store. The tableau came undone; the three subjects turned towards her. Madame Jodoin straightened up, a little white card in her hand. "They just got in some real nice pillowcases, come and see!"

The reply came in spite of her, expelling part of her rage like a stream of vomit.

"He can take his goddamn pillowcases and shove them up his ass!"

After brushing off the knees of his pants as best he could, he washed his hands energetically. The muddy water ran into the sink, swirled around the drain for a moment, then disappeared with an ugly sucking sound. Every thirty seconds you could hear the flushing of the urinals that lined the wall. There was a strong smell of mothballs.

Jay Pee Jodoin, who had followed him in, was leaning against one of the big porcelain sinks, hands knotted behind his head, legs crossed.

"I don't know what it's about, all he said was he wanted to find you.... He asked me and I'm not even in your class.... Claude said you took off pretty fast after the exam...."

"You didn't say anything to Frère...."

"How could I, I didn't know where you were! I didn't even know you'd disappeared! Where were you anyway?"

"Never mind.... The less you know the better...."

Jay Pee, wounded, straightened up and came and stood next to his friend.

"What's that supposed to mean? I can't keep a secret? Is that it? You think I'll go and spill the beans to the teacher? That's how you thank me when I do you a favour and tell you he's looking for you so you can cook up an excuse before he nabs you?"

The fat woman's child shook his hands over the sink, took a brown paper towel from the holder and meticulously dried them.

"Quit complaining all the time, you sound like Claude! Where is he anyway? Bawling his eyes out in the corner so we'll feel sorry for him? He failed his exam so I suppose it's everybody's fault but his!"

There was something different about him, but Jay Pee couldn't grasp what it was. Maybe it was the way he talked to him, the germ of contempt that was new and nasty, that he could sense beneath the mocking words, the kind of irritation a superior feels towards his guilty subordinate. The fat woman's child had become condescending all at once and Jay Pee was deeply shocked.

The other boy aimed at the wastebasket and missed. His crumpled towel landed in the corner of the room.

In a pitiful attempt to be condescending in turn, Jay Pee shrugged his shoulders.

"You're no good at sports I guess, you can't even hit a target!"

"You can't either...but with words, not paper!"

Again! Jay Pee, feeling ashamed and, yes, unable to come up with a reply, stuffed his hands in his pockets and stared at his toes.

The fat woman's child took a good long look at himself in the big mirror over the wash-basins, to be sure he was clean and that no sign remained of his visit to the enchanted forest.

Jay Pee took advantage of that pause to react, and he clipped his friend on the back of his head.

"Don't worry, you're beautiful...."

He felt an urge to shake him up, to be mean to him with some remark like, "Who do you think you are all of a sudden, you never used to talk to me like that and you sure aren't going to start now," but curiosity won out. Even if he didn't like the tone of the fat woman's child, he wanted to know where he'd been.

"Where were you anyway? We looked all over! You weren't in the schoolyard, you weren't in the can.... I even went up to the third floor to see if you were playing 'Corridor sans issue' but all the class-rooms were empty.... You didn't leave the schoolyard, did you? You know you could end up being tortured in Thumbless Buddha's office for the rest of the after-noon!"

Turning abruptly towards Jay Pee to tell him off again, the fat woman's child got a glimpse of the Vice Principal's silhouette coming their way. He'd be in the toilet any second. To save them from a gaffe that could cost them dearly because Saint-Stanislas pupils weren't allowed to hang around the bathrooms during recess, the boy decided to exaggerate his irritation, and he elbowed Jay Pee very hard.

"Mind your own business and quit following me around like a shadow! Can't I even have constipation?"

He acted as if he hadn't seen the brother and dived in, almost bouncing off the Vice Principal's gen-erous pot-belly. He didn't give him a chance to say anything either.

"Hey, make him leave me alone! I was just ...just...anyway, I was in the stall and I was straining and he starts saying everybody's looking for me! He kept saying I had to come out and I couldn't finish what I was doing! Is everybody really looking for me?"

All at once Jay Pee turned pale and froze there, leaning against the big sink. No one had ever dared to use that tone of voice with Thumbless Buddha, the terror of Saint-Stanislas, the strap-wielding maniac, specialist in using the triangular ruler on your knuckles, the one readers of the works of Captain Johns called "the escaped German Nazi." When he heard himself speak, the fat woman's child thought, *That's it, this time I went too far, he's going to raise that ugly great big hand without a thumb and give me a smack on the jaw that'll leave my face puffed up till Saint-Jean-Baptiste Day....* He was already starting to blink like someone expecting to be hit at any moment, but he didn't even dare to hide behind his folded arm — a move Thumbless Buddha particularly despised and was always overjoyed to punish.

But nothing happened, no slaps, no threats. They stood there silently for a few seconds. All the urinals flushed at once. Very slowly the Vice Principal brought up his hand (the one without the thumb, in fact, the one malicious gossips claimed he'd lost up the ass of a particularly obliging Grade Nine boy, but you didn't have to believe them), stopping it, however, at waist level, where he usually concealed his missing thumb in the row of buttons on his soutane. His voice was so calm the fat woman's child felt lost: the Vice Principal's temper tantrums were preferable to this false equanimity.

"You know very well you aren't allowed here during recess. It's *strictly* forbidden!"

So the Vice Principal was going to use argument instead of violence, which was very rare and very worrying: They could spend hours and hours repeating the same questions and the same answers over and over until the boy snapped and confessed everything. It didn't matter what, just everything. If he didn't act quickly, if he didn't provoke Thumbless Buddha's anger in the next few seconds, he was going to launch into one of those famous but rare inquisitions and he'd get him in the end by wearing him down.

And the boy decided to stake his all and jump into trouble with both feet.

"I can't control when I have to go! I thought it couldn't wait but it could, so it was really a false alarm! But I'm pretty sure everything would start moving if you hit me! But I warn you, it won't be my fault if you end up covered in shit!"

He heard, he *really* heard Peter Pan laughing in one of the stalls. The throaty laugh of an adolescent who's just heard a good dirty joke — or told one. He bit back the smile he could feel coming to his lips. Whatever was going to happen, punishment, blows, insults or threats of expulsion, he knew that he'd done the right thing because Peter Pan was laughing. He looked up at the Vice Principal's face. He was going to hold his gaze (another absolute rule at Saint-Stanislas: always look down when a teacher is chewing you out), yes, he'd hold his gaze to show he wasn't afraid of him: *Go ahead, give me the strap, I don't care, I'm not afraid any more, I've got my other self, the one that has fun, and my other self's going to keep on having fun even if you make me bleed, even if you make me pass out like Jacques Bolduc last year!* But his heart tightened in his chest, he felt his legs go weak under him and he had to lean against the door-frame.

It wasn't Peter Pan who was laughing now.

The Vice Principal's laughter rose above the sound of the flushing, it filled the bathroom of the École Saint-Stanislas, it reverberated in a kind of instantaneous echo that increased its strength tenfold; surely it would smash the walls of the room, spread

into the schoolyard and over the whole neighbourhood; Montreal would hear this laughter that had
come out of the wrong mouth and everyone would
know that a poor child in the Plateau Mont-Royal had
mistaken it for that of his idol, his refuge, his alter ego.
The mistake was so ridiculous, so pitiful, a tremendous
fatigue struck him somewhere in his chest. The fatigue
wasn't physical, it was as if his emotions had gone into
neutral and a kind of fatalism was creeping over him.
He felt as if everything in him was abdicating and he
wanted to cry, perhaps to provide a tragic counterpart
for Thumbless Buddha's grotesque laughter. From the
corner of his eye he could see Peter Pan leave the
bathroom, sticking his tongue out.

The Vice Principal was doubled over. He held his
belly in both hands, then wiped the tears that were
pouring down his cheek. He looked as if he'd still be
there in two hours, tomorrow, next year, indefinitely,
like the fat lady at Belmont Park who terrorized all the
children.

The boy pushed him aside, gently, so he could
leave the room.

Jay Pee, paler than ever, followed him. The afternoon sun struck them full in the forehead. Already,
Frère Robert was gesturing to the fat woman's child
that he wanted to talk to him. They pretended they
couldn't see him and sat on the cement guardrail
along the steps going down to the schoolyard. Jay Pee
gestured in Thumbless Buddha's direction.

"Some people are closer to the apes than others,
eh?"

Marcel was lying on his back. His aunt had given him permission to get into his mother's bed, something she did whenever he had a seizure, as if she knew that he had had one. She hadn't asked a single question when he emerged from the bathroom half an hour later, bored to death and with the shape of the toilet seat imprinted on his buttocks; she merely told him quietly to lie down in his mother's room. That was a reward and it shocked him. She smoothed the dish towels she'd taken from the clothesline for Albertine to iron later. He wished he could have refused her gift with a few succinct words, knocked over the pile of towels, slammed the door yelling that he'd never come back, thrown a tantrum — pointless, but what a relief — but how could he resist his mother's bed?

He looked up at the ceiling. The plaster molding around the frosted glass light fixture, the woodwork his uncle Gabriel had painted bottle-green one day when he came home from work with some leftover paint nobody wanted; the cracks, bigger and bigger and more and more a cause for concern, that ran in every direction and made his mother say she was going to wake up murdered by a coat of plaster one of these days. It smelled good. It smelled of her, when she was resting, when the day's trials and tribulations were over or hadn't yet begun. Unlike the fat woman's child, Marcel could smell no trace of a man's presence in his mother's bed; his father had gone away to the war when he was very young and he'd hardly known him; no, it just smelled of her in the only position from which she didn't yell at him: flat on her back.

He closed his eyes. Not to sleep — he'd slept enough for today — but to be permeated through as many senses as possible with everything that had to do with Albertine when she was lying here, snoring or breathing peacefully, agitated or calm, one leg out of the covers, an arm folded across her forehead if the light reached her there. The sense of smell was easy, it came by itself, he just had to take a deep breath and there she was. Touch wasn't too hard either: He could simply run his hands over the chenille spread and the coolness of the pillow. As for hearing, there he had to use his imagination: It was late at night, he'd just come back after having a pee, he wasn't completely awake; a funny sound came from his mother's bedroom; he stuck his head in the door that was open a crack — and he had hearing and seeing at the same time! It was one of those nights when she'd over-indulged in greasy *cretons* or fixed herself a cucumber sandwich before bedtime and now you could hear her all over the house. The next day, Gabriel or the fat woman would talk knowingly about the late-night concert that had kept everybody awake, but Albertine pretended she didn't know what they were talking about. Taste was the hardest. Can you taste your own mother? He had tried to, once. At night, needless to say. When she was snoring. He'd approached quietly, bent over her foot that was sticking out of the bed, he'd pressed his lips against the skin and put out his tongue. It tasted of soap. Just like when he made a bruise on his own arm by puckering his lips and sucking. So now he knew everything about his mother when she was lying in her bed, except how she tasted. Maybe the backs of her knees, or under her arms...somewhere else, too, in those forbidden areas you weren't supposed to think about even if it was getting harder not to, she might taste of something that was specific to her. Herself. He slowly raised his arm, moved his head down, sniffed. His cotton shirt smelled of sweat. He always smelled of sweat, everybody said so. Sweat, and unwashed little boy. She washed herself too much for his liking and not enough for hers.

He was overcome by uneasiness as he looked up at the ceiling. That feeling was becoming very familiar but he did his best to ignore it because he didn't understand it. His penis had stiffened while he was sniffing his armpit. He raised himself up on one elbow. It made a bump in his pants. This was happening more and more often, in places that were more and more embarrassing. At school all the boys it happened to laughed at it. Some were already speaking highly about masturbation and had the circles under their eyes to vouch for it. As a topic of conversation it was especially satisfying because it made the girls blush. But until now Marcel had never dared to touch his stiff penis. He suffered the turmoil it set off in him and waited for it to pass. But this time he wanted something else, he wanted to experience the violence, then the relief and even the depressing sense of guilt that break over you afterwards, that all his classmates talked about (because all of it, don't try to deny it, was very ugly in spite of the pleasure it gave you, and a very serious sin).

But wouldn't his aunt barge in, wouldn't his mother come back from Schiller's and catch him doing the shameful deed? Why do it here, in her bed? Why not go back to the toilet? After all, it was one of the things that happen in that part of your body, that go on in the secluded room where nobody else is allowed when you're inside...

But the urge, the *desire* — yes, the nearly unbearable desire — was too powerful. This was no time for rationalization: His aunt and his mother wouldn't catch him in the act, they couldn't! He undid the buttons of his fly, then the one that fastened his pants around his waist. He separated the tails of his shirt, pulled down his pants, his underwear. His penis was throbbing, as if something alive was shaking it a little. He looked at it for a long moment, as if it had nothing to do with him, didn't belong to him. But it belonged to him all right, because his desire kept growing. He wanted to take hold of his penis and agitate it from top to bottom (that's what the others had told him to do) but something, probably a black thread that had come loose from his pants, drew his attention to his pubis. He pulled the thread to brush it away but it resisted, and he felt a little pinch. A long black nearly curly hair had grown in next to his penis, something so indecent, so much *more* indecent than his erection, he was flabbergasted. He bent over a little more. There were little bits of hair, black roots like the ones he'd seen on his cousins and his uncle Gabriel in the morning, all over the area around his penis. He was growing a beard down there!

He howled as he got out of his mother's bed and started to jump up and down in the bedroom like someone who has just caught sight of an abomination from hell.

"I don't want it! I don't want that! I don't want it! I don't want it!"

The Beau Coq Bar-B-Q on Mont-Royal had recently replaced an old butcher shop where for many years products forbidden by law had been sold under the counter (mainly horse meat that people came from as far away as Outremont or Westmount to buy). On Monday morning in particular, when limousines were lined up outside the expensive and exclusive Mont-Royal Convent just across the street, you'd see ladies in hats or chauffeurs in livery emerge from the butcher shop clutching small brown paper packages containing the forbidden meat. The city had eventually shut down the butcher shop and now nobody but young students emerged from the limousines on Monday mornings.

The Beau Coq Bar-B-Q was an establishment trying to be chic and tasteful: soft lighting, few ornaments, a sloping ceiling to look modern, dark walls to look rich, nearly inaudible music. But as soon as you were inside, the goal of looking distinguished on this street where greasy French fries and the omnipresent hot dog prevailed was negated by the huge plaster rooster, spurs out and neck stretched in a silent cock-a-doodle-doo, surmounted by a gigantic lampshade of imitation straw — a hideous lamp in aggressive colours that frightened the children and would have been right at home in the tackiest five-and-dime store. In addition, this masterpiece of bad taste was perched on a wrought-iron column laced with climbing vines, busy bees, and classical acanthus leaves. And so it was a Corinthian column crowned by a Gallic rooster that greeted the customers from Plateau Mont-Royal whenever they had a craving for barbecued chicken. It took up a lot of room and it created a powerful effect. The day manager, Monsieur Dubé, thought that most of all, it looked serious.

Inside the restaurant, after being slightly startled by the plaster rooster, Albertine asked the pudgy gentleman, the aforementioned Monsieur Dubé, who was coming towards her: "What's going on, is it open or closed? You can't see a thing in here!"

With a stiff, contemptuous little smile, he ushered her to a table at the very back, in the darkest part of the room where the undesirables were seated. She had slightly overdone her reluctance to edge herself onto the banquette so he'd know that you really couldn't see a thing in his goddamn restaurant.

"Good thing you came back here with me, I'd've got lost on my own!"

He held out a menu she couldn't have read if she'd wanted to.

"Where's Thérèse? I'm her mother."

He took the menu from her with an exasperated sigh and disappeared towards the kitchen, muttering something about personal visits to employees.

Albertine looked around, squinting; she realized she was the only customer in this place that was too expensive for her and decided she'd never set foot in here again, even if her daughter worked here for years. A plain old drumstick must cost a mint!

She had come here to console herself over Mr. Schiller's profligacy and already sensed that she'd made a bad choice. Again. She'd have been wiser to go for a smoked-meat sandwich at the Three Minute Lunch or a chicken fried rice at the Café Asia — they were more her speed and she was used to them. There, she would know what attitude to assume, what to order and how to eat it, whereas here.... She parked her purse on the table, decided it was too big, dropped it onto the banquette beside her, opened it, took out a handkerchief, and wiped her lips, *Otherwise my lunch will taste like lipstick...*, and turned when she heard her daughter come out of the kitchen.

Thérèse had been working here for a few months now and she raved about the food: "You'll see, the chicken's practically better than yours!" (supreme insult); and the clientele: "No poor shoe salesmen, just store managers and bank managers! Even Monsieur Allard who doesn't talk to anybody on our street though he's a neighbour, he eats his lunch there with his colleagues from the bank!" Albertine thought to herself that maybe bank managers preferred not to see what was on their plates.... Her daughter had also told her how nice the day shift boss was, the same Monsieur Dubé, and the other waitresses (for Thérèse to say anything good about the people she worked with was already an event) and told her to drop in whenever she wanted for some nicely roasted chicken with good French fries and wonderful Bar-B-Q sauce.

So here she was. And wishing she were anywhere else.

The lie was easily spotted, fun to develop, and juicy to repeat.

Frère Robert had started by walking down the rows of seats in Grade Four C to say that he wanted to talk to him. This time the fat woman's child had lowered his eyes. Above all he didn't want his teacher to see that he wasn't afraid of him any more. Or of anything. He wanted to play the lamb with the lamb, after being the lion with the lion. He even tried to blush but couldn't do it. The self-confidence, the arrogance even that he hadn't experienced before and had been very happy to discover in the school washroom just now, let him glimpse other prospects hitherto undreamed-of. His fairly easy victory over the terror of Saint-Stanislas had temporarily erased from his memory his defeat in the enchanted forest; depression had given way to exaltation; he suddenly felt smarter, shrewder, stronger, deliberately forgetting that he had acted on the spur of the moment, without preparation, thinking naïvely that now that he'd got a laugh out of Thumbless Buddha, when he'd never even suspected the man knew how to, he could do anything.

So he had had two minutes, just long enough to go to his classroom and cook up some excuse for his disappearance after the geography exam. A good explanation, a solid reason that would stand up even if he landed in the principal's office. But he wasn't worried. He'd think of something, as he had just now; he'd improvise, and everything would work out. From now on he was invincible.

Claude Lemieux leaned across to him and said out of the corner of his mouth, "Boy, you're really going to get it now!"

The fat woman's child looked him squarely in the eyes.

"Jeez, you sound as if you're glad!"

That was when he noticed, behind his friend's head, the grey silhouette of the Saint-Stanislas church on the other side of de Lanaudière. And even before the rows of Grade Four C began to get out of their seats, he had found his lie. He made a triumphant entrance into the school, grinning from ear to ear as he revisited the bathroom where the Vice Principal's laughter still echoed, blithely climbing the marble stairs: He wasn't on his way to the scaffold now as Claude Lemieux seemed to hope, he was heading for another victory.

Frère Robert kept him in the corridor while the other pupils were getting ready for the last exam of the day. And the fat woman's child, with disconcerting ease and violent pleasure, confessed his "sin." Leaning against the wall in the corridor, he told his story in a voice filled with fake emotion, fake excitement. Anxious at the thought of failing that morning's exam, he had quickly disposed of Geography, which was really easy and so inconsequential, to get ready for the math exam that had him a little scared. And to prepare himself properly, yes, he admitted it, he'd gone outside the limits of the school. But just to go into the church! He had run across the street, trembling, he'd entered into the smell of stale incense, he had thrown himself on his knees at the communion table and offered up his life, his soul, to God. He spent a wonderful hour there and God, yes, he had sensed Him there, as if he'd heard His voice. And God had reassured him: He was a good boy, he'd been right to go outside the limits of the school and come here to confide in Him, he would probably pass his exams if he continued to concentrate.

It was as big as a mountain and so unbelievable it verged on the ridiculous but he was convinced it would work because while he was telling it *he himself was convinced.* He believed everything he said: He watched himself acting as he'd already done three times today, but this time he could control his actions and his thoughts because he was inventing them; he was creating from start to finish a truth that was incredible but to which he was able to give a whiff of credibility because he believed it. His lie was perfectly sincere: He was learning how to tell a well-turned lie, embellished with a thousand details, acted out with just enough emotion, sufficiently restrained to make the other person believe he was being let in on a secret, and peremptory when that person had to be convinced there was a sound reason for what he'd done; he was "acting" for the first time in his life and it gave him a feeling of jubilation that was hard to contain. Frère Robert couldn't resist such "sincerity." And he didn't.

The fat woman's child saw his teacher's face transformed as he developed his story, polished the details: the smell inside the church, the sound, the light from the stained-glass windows on the walls, his soul opening up, his joy when he realized he'd been listened to, heard.... In the space of a few minutes Frère Robert's expression went from anger to doubt, from doubt to amazement, from amazement to comprehension, and from comprehension to a kind of ingratiating admiration that his pupil was extremely pleased to have created by means of a successful demeanor on his face and convincing words.

For a few moments though he thought he was lost: either he'd laid it on too thick or a remark was badly worded, so when Frère Robert frowned he nearly slipped. He'd started to tell about glimpsing a shadow near the high altar, an ethereal form that had vanished as soon as he looked at it, but when he saw the look on his teacher's face he realized he mustn't go *too* far, he *must not* venture onto the slippery ground of apparitions: He risked losing everything if he went too far. He quickly landed on his feet, made the mysterious shadow cough and become the beadle who was busy doing something or other, and he was safe: He had "dreamed" of an apparition because he was in the church praying, which was ridiculous but perfectly normal. Frère Robert smiled at this understandable weakness and the fat woman's child was very relieved.

Until then his fantasies had always put him inside the character of Peter Pan; he'd told himself stories when he needed them, to forget his problems, to get through difficult moments, or simply because he loved to daydream, but he had never tried them out on anyone else. Oh, he'd made up a tall tale for his friends last summer and he was going to do the same thing this year, but his friends knew they were jokes to help them get through rainy afternoons, knew that none of them were true, that they came from his natural talent as a storyteller he'd gotten from his great-uncle Josaphat-le-violon, that they were unlikely to have any repercussions; now, though, to cover up the fact that he'd run away, to save his hide, he was risking the first big lie of his life, and he was thrilled at how successful he could be. He told himself that from now on this would be his only system of defense. Against everything. And everybody. If Marcel really experienced wonderful things that nobody else believed, he was going to invent others, not as crazy but more pernicious, that would fool them all. He was going to become, he already was, a cheat.

Frère Robert, more moved than he wanted to show, ushered him into the classroom where the other pupils were waiting more or less in silence.

"That sauce is way too strong! It burnt my tongue!"

Thérèse looked up from the pile of paper napkins she was folding.

"You don't have to eat it, Ma! I only wanted you to taste! It's something new! God almighty, can't I even give you a treat without you complaining?"

After she'd downed half of her Coke, making too much fuss about how badly she needed it, Albertine pushed the bowl of sauce towards the salt and pepper shakers at the end of the table.

"Probably some of your customers can't even talk! My mouth's on fire!"

"You already said that...."

"And my eyes are watering! I didn't say anything about that...."

She tucked into the French fries and thought they were delicious, crisp the way she liked them, especially those that were charred, and chewed away while she observed something amazing: For Thérèse to be placidly folding paper napkins in the middle of the afternoon, in a restaurant on Plateau Mont-Royal, was almost inconceivable, an unfathomable mystery. Thérèse was rebellious, a woman of action, foulmouthed, high-living, a nightclub waitress who could carry a dozen beers and not drop one, even when the customers tried to grab her legs, not someone who waited on tables in a Bar-B-Q joint and folded napkins while she waited for the supper hour rush!

What could have changed her? Albertine wished she could rejoice to see her daughter settling down, but a sense of doubt warned her not to get too excited too fast, not to freeze Thérèse into permanently doing some repetitive task that was so unlike her. Unless, of course, there was a good reason for it. But what could have convinced Thérèse to leave the nightlife of the Main to bury herself here in the middle of the afternoon, at an hour when she was usually still sleeping off the night before?

Albertine stopped chewing a crisp, delicious piece of skin. Actually, there was just one reason for a nightclub waitress to settle down. After a brief moment of sheer amazement, she checked an urge to lean across the table, hold out her arms to her daughter, and ask her for a big juicy kiss....

A baby! Thérèse was expecting a baby, that must be it! Nothing else could bring about such a change. She was going to be a grandmother! Thérèse's good-for-nothing husband Gérard had finally produced something! Mr. Schiller was forgotten, along with the rest of her troubles, the rest of her life; she saw herself on the balcony on Fabre Street with a bundle of cotton and wool in her arms, glad to be rocking something besides her own miseries, too long mulled over, too often ruminated. She saw herself next summer, the baby — boy, girl, it didn't matter — was a few months old, and she was looking after it during the daytime because Thérèse was placidly folding paper napkins at the Beau Coq Bar-B-Q.... It was *her* baby and everything, absolutely everything in her life had changed dramatically. And she was happy.

But the dream was short-lived. Thérèse lit a cigarette — a Turret, the most dangerous kind, the strongest, the ones that smelled the worst and made you cough — took a long drag, then looked at her mother.

"I'm getting the hell out of here. I'm sick of standing around with my mouth hanging open and besides, you can't make any money. Those bank managers are a bunch of cheapskates; they think a compliment between their chicken sandwich and dessert is as good as a tip, and they bugger off and don't leave you one red cent. I'm going back to the French Casino with Pierrette, and I don't want to hear a word about it!"

Albertine almost asked: "What about your baby?" but she caught herself just in time. Thérèse hadn't changed. Nothing had changed. Her dream of escape had lasted the length of time it took to chew some chicken skin. She picked up a piece of dark meat that was too big and too greasy and she felt as if it was going to make her gag.

Thérèse continued talking, but very quietly, as if she were carrying on a monologue to convince herself that what she had to say was right. She rolled her cigarette along the edge of the ashtray, tapped it nervously to shake off ash that hadn't yet had time to form, chewing at it or holding it very straight between her teeth when she was searching for her words. Albertine didn't look at her daughter's face; she was following her hand, the swirls of smoke, she was watching the pile of compressed napkins grow higher and trying to predict when they'd fall off the table. And she'd stopped eating. Chicken and fries were congealing on her plate and a greasy skin was settling over the sauce beside the salt and pepper.

"This can't go on. If I stay here I'll go crazy and you'll have to put me away.... I can't live like this.... Peace and quiet aren't my style. This place is stifling me. When it's two o'clock in the afternoon and there isn't a goddamn soul in sight and I know I won't see a customer till five-thirty, I want to wreck the place! I need noise, I need action and cigarette smoke and the smell of beer and booze.... I'm made for getting rid of the girls that walk across the stage and for discouraging hands under the tables.... I want the night. That's where I want to work. And live. I'm made for nightlife. For leaving the French Casino when it's starting to get light, with Pierrette and Simone still counting their change...and having one last drink with them, the one that knocks me out so I can forget that daytime exists.... In here, everything's upside down for me. I did my best to get the hell away from Plateau Mont-Royal, I married a jerk who tried to shut me up in a one-bedroom apartment on Dorion Street, I talked him into letting me go to work before I killed him, I ended up on the Main and got back in touch with the ones who really *had* got the hell out...my only real friends, Pierrette and Simone, your brother, my uncle Édouard, who's the life of the party on the Main, Maurice who wants people to take him seriously as a pimp, but you can remind him what's what with a slap in the face...people like me, people that think like me, that live like me, at night, people that drink and laugh till they finally forget they're alive. I don't want to come back here and dish out Bar-B-Q to people I hate because they look down on me. I tried. Because I was weak. And tired. Sure, I'm tired now, but it's worse when I stop, I know that. Why keep trying to tell myself it suits me here. I'm miserable! On the Main, when my legs went as limp as rags I'd knock back a good stiff drink and I'd go on. This place is killing me. I'm dead here. From boredom. Because here it feels like I'm working to earn my living. But that's not why I work on the Main...."

She stopped in mid-sentence. She tried for a few seconds to finish it but couldn't find the words. She ground out the stub of cigarette that was starting to burn her fingers.

"On the Main, I don't work. I think what I do is have fun."

At the word "fun" Albertine started.

"Wait and see if you're still having fun when you're twenty-five and look fifty."

Thérèse smiled. Just a hint of a sad little smile.

"You've been a hundred all your life, Ma. And you've never had any fun at all. I intend to go on having fun forever."

Her daughter's naïveté made Albertine jump off her seat.

"I've heard enough for today.... Let me know when you've got something else to tell me...."

She walked away, tugging at her dress and clutching her purse under her left arm. She was muttering to herself things she'd turned over a hundred times, things she didn't dare say to Thérèse here in this fancy restaurant, because of the danger that the ensuing fight would turn Monsieur Dubé's shiny clean ears red. "Fun! What kind of fun? Serving drunks and floozies who don't even know what they're saying? Or spending all night with a grin on your face because they put something in your drink to make you even drunker because their drinks aren't strong enough, aren't strong enough to keep you on your feet? Or keeping a pillow over your head all day because the light hurts your eyes? What kind of fun is that?" She nearly bumped into the plaster rooster as she walked past it, and she was already pulling on the door to leave when she heard her daughter's voice in the dark depths of the restaurant.

"I can't even remember your phone number!"

Never in ten years had he found the door locked. He could always climb up the three steps to the gallery without worrying that he'd have to make himself known in some way before he could get inside: On the worst day of a heat wave, when everything in Montreal was asleep and only the cicadas' stridulations pierced the sticky humidity, or after a snowstorm, in the muffled stillness of Fabre Street sleeping under two feet of snow, he just had to push the door and it would open onto those perfumes of another age that assailed him as soon as he was inside, onto those sounds they had taught him to produce as well as to appreciate, onto that light that had nothing to do with the weather outside, onto those women who were always the same, eternally young and eternally old, interchangeable but terribly different, at once serious and happy, who had taken his life in their hands and had guided him, the solitary and different child, towards knowledge as disturbing as it was vast, and to his cat. Behind it all, knowledge both intellectual and sensual, there had always been the clown-like mentor who could teach him, between two sessions of cuddling or two naps on the apron of the stove, words as long as your arm and undreamed-of concepts that he had the ability to make simple and comprehensible.

They were the incarnation of all the knowledge that had existed since the beginning of time, which he, a ball of fur, transmitted. And Marcel, in a rapture that had never failed in ten years, had been the receptacle wherein the most beautiful, the most precious things were deposited.

But on this breathtakingly sumptuous late afternoon, when the brand-new summer was unfurling her first sweltering heat, the door was locked.

Marcel had run down the stairs of his house, his pants badly buttoned, his unwanted erection still fondling his leg, skin of penis against skin of thigh, in a way that excited him. His desire was still just as keen, but the disgust he'd felt at the sight of the black hair on his pubis kept him from thrusting his hand inside his pants to relieve himself. Because that was what he needed to do. For the first time. Though he knew how to look at art and how to talk about it, aware of the five senses which he could name without an error, he knew nothing about the true secrets of nature, didn't know that his body, probably under cover of night, would relieve itself of its excess of sap on its own if he didn't do it himself, and he thought that what was happening between his legs, this transformation he'd have gladly done without, would last forever. He saw himself sauntering through life with a bump in his pants that he couldn't get rid of, and he was ashamed.

His friends at school, even the girls, had often talked about it in his presence, in fact he was the last boy to whom it was happening, the others having long since been practising that wonderful relief, mysterious and forbidden, blushing as they brutally described it. Deep down, then, he knew it was temporary, knew the bump would go away and then come back, but in the panic of the moment, especially because of the hair growing down there, which his friends had never mentioned, and because of his heart as well, that was pounding as it did when he'd been running too fast, though all he'd done now was descend the stairs, his mind went blank and he couldn't think beyond his erection.

At the bottom of the staircase he bent over in case he should run into anyone, and slipped as quickly as he could into the neighbours' front yard. He sat on their front stoop thinking that, after all, he couldn't appear like that in front of them, who had never told him anything about what goes on below the belt. He waited, head bowed. Anyone passing by would have thought he was praying, a good little Catholic devoting a few minutes of his time to his God.

His heart calmed down. Slowly, with a sensation of warmth that disturbed him, the bump gradually shrank. Something sticky slipped onto his thigh, cutting it in two as if blood had flowed from a wound. He waited to be quite sure his penis was back inside his underwear before he straightened up.

Should he tell them about it? The mere thought made him blush violently. No. He'd keep it quiet and let himself be lulled by today's lesson. Or by the demonstration of some other useless wonder.

He saw his reflection in the glass of the door. A gangling adolescent, staggering slightly, his back already bowed by chronic guilt; a once-beautiful child who had been given everything and was now beginning to lose his footing under the weight of so much ill-digested, poorly channelled knowledge.

He turned the doorknob without thinking, as he'd

been doing for so long. It took him a few seconds to realize it wasn't going to open, because it was locked. During those few seconds he turned the knob again and again, pushed the door without really thinking of anything. Then all at once the truth came to him and for a brief moment he felt as if he was going to spend the rest of his life vainly pushing this door while watching his reflection in the glass grow older.

And then for the first time he saw the doorbell, on his right. Had it always been there? Or had it loomed out of nothingness to show him that from now on he must ask permission to gain access to the treasures inside this house that were forbidden to everyone but him? He straightened his index finger, hesitated, then gently pressed the metallic button, probably brass, highly polished in any case. A little click, the door comes ajar. But only slightly. Just room enough for two ears pointed towards him, two eyes sparkling with mischief, a cold wet muzzle, and bushy whiskers.

The door closed. Another click.

But Duplessis was there.

"They're doing it on purpose, I know they are! They want everybody in Grade Four in Quebec to repeat their year! Next year there'll be lots and lots of kids in Grade Four and nobody in Grade Five! There'll be sixty pupils in every Grade Four class and Grade Five will be empty! There'll be empty classrooms all over the school but the Grade Fours will be so crowded we'll all suffocate to death! I bet they don't have enough Grade Five teachers! What are we supposed to do when they start asking questions about stuff we've never heard of? When you don't even understand the words in the question, what words do you use in your answers? I left all kinds of blanks on my paper when I handed it in to Frère Robert. All I did was underline the words in the questions I didn't know and put a question mark on top! At least they'll see it wasn't because I didn't know the answers, it was the questions I didn't understand! You guys, the smart ones, you probably understood everything, right? You, you go away and then turn up again like Our Lord Jesus Christ, did you know what that word 'symonym' on the exam this morning meant?"

"It isn't symonym it's sy*n*onym...."

"So what? What difference does that make? I still don't understand! You already correct me on the words I understand, if you start on the ones that I don't...."

Claude Lemieux was red with anger. And dry-eyed. The fat woman's child and Jay Pee Jodoin had expected to see him leave the class in tears because the math exam had been particularly hard, but he seemed to have exhausted his stock for the day. His cheeks were blazing, his forehead damp, but his eyes showed no trace of moisture, in fact they were streaked with red like someone who's just left a smoke-filled room with eyelids stinging.

"I'm glad I'm not coming back next year! You're all sick!"

There was a slight hesitation. Claude Lemieux looked at his two friends, not understanding what was going on, then all at once he realized the implications of what he'd just said and like a fountain shut off for the winter, whose valves you open to see if everything is working properly, tears suddenly welled up, generous and sincere, because they arose not from rage but from genuine pain, pain that came from his heart.

So what if he was going on to Grade Five? He wouldn't know anybody where he was going! He'd be surrounded by hostile strangers who'd polish him off in no time, the way the Big Bad Wolf had done to Little Red Riding Hood in the expurgated version the fat woman's child had told him, that had kept him from sleeping for a whole week....

An image came to him: It's Monday, the first day of classes...he arrives at the school...it's ugly, run down, standing in a deserted field...it has taken him two and a half hours to walk here...in the rain...he goes into the schoolyard full of country hicks with their boots covered with...what do you call it, with...anyhow, with cow shit...there is silence...they all turn to look at him in his cute little powder blue short pants he's ashamed to wear even in the city, they make him look like such a sissy...they all start laughing...the hicks with their boots covered with...come at him with scary looks on their faces...and his calvary is beginning.

That was the image that made him start to cry, much more because of himself and his own tremendous unhappiness than over the loss of his friends. Even though he adored them all, not so much for what they were as for what they'd always given him in spite of all their teasing: emotional security, primitive affection that was rarely expressed but real. He had known them forever, they were his family, and the mere thought that he was going to be without that family in what might be a hostile environment made him wild with fear. As a perfectly selfish nine-year-old he was the centre of his own universe and everything else, even humans, was incidental and served only his own well-being; these people existed to take care of him, and what would become of him among others who till now had existed without him? Would he be accepted in someone else's puzzle, or be rejected like a piece of blue sky that has found its way into a jigsaw depicting a forest in autumn? All that went through his mind at the same time: the strange school; the mocking laughter of new classmates who would never be his family; his own puzzle, with himself as the central piece, the keystone; the other one that showed a drawing he wasn't part of, from which he would probably be banished. And he wept.

As for Jay Pee Jodoin, he wasn't displeased with himself: An average student, he always aimed for average marks and was satisfied with average results, which spared him the worries and torments of students who work too hard or the false complacency of dunces who don't give a damn — or pretend they don't at any rate. Unlike Claude Lemieux, he hadn't panicked over the difficulties in the French or math exams. He'd begun by setting aside the questions he didn't understand (he didn't know what a synonym was either) so he could concentrate on the others. Then he'd answered the easiest questions and slogged away during the rest of the period over the traps he thought he could avoid. Which pretty well guaranteed him the sixty percent he needed to pass.

In fact, he moved through everything in life with a lack of ambition and enterprise that made him even-tempered, never very angry but never enthusiastic either, just charming enough, not a follower but not a gang leader either, who would be seen as happy when things were going well, but not really devastated if they turned bad.

He wasn't lethargic or passive, no, he'd always been the first to run, to climb, to hide in the unlikeliest places when they were playing kick the can or racking their brains on rainy days when it was time to concentrate on guessing games. But he never instigated anything either: Others had to decide for him that it was time to run, to climb, to hide, to guess.... He had the placidity of one who expects nothing special from life and is content to watch it pass without really getting involved. His father, for instance, dreamed that he'd become a bus driver like him, and Jay Pee would think, *Why not, it's not so bad and it's better than lots of other jobs....*

Almost reassured now that he'd passed his math exam, he'd have liked to run out of the school, forget about the other exams waiting for him next Monday and concentrate on the weekend, but he had to console Claude Lemieux who was panicking and sniffling like a two-year-old, and so he did what he could to console him, showing neither exasperation nor compassion. The time for forgetting and games would be here eventually so why hurry, why get impatient....

As for the fat woman's child, he was seething with impatience. He'd really had enough of his friend's weeping and moaning, and he caught himself looking forward to the time when he'd be out of his life for good. He liked Claude and knew he'd miss him when he moved to Saint-Eustache, but right now, right here at the door to the school, in the middle of the empty schoolyard, under this blazing sun that summoned up everything except lamentations, he felt like shaking him, pinching him, pushing him, knocking him down....

"If you did some studying now and then you wouldn't have so much to cry about! They could wash the schoolyard with the tears you've shed today and I'm not kidding!"

He knew perfectly well how unfair that was: His friend worked, he worked hard, he managed to learn through sheer force of will and hard work, but he was also a bundle of nerves who forgot everything as soon as he was in any situation where he was unsure of himself — and everything, absolutely everything in life seemed unsure to him the minute he was outside his mother's house. If the school were moved to his house, he'd be at the head of his class!

Claude Lemieux raised himself on tiptoe the way short people do when they're insulted.

"One of these days you'll tell me you miss my crying!"

"You're dumber than I thought! How can I tell you that, you won't be here?"

Shrill laughter burst out near by and the three boys turned their heads. Three girls were waiting for them at the gate of the schoolyard, Carmen Brassard and Carmen Ouimet arm-in-arm, Linda Lauzon with her finger deep in her right nostril. The absurdity of the tableau — three girls in the boys' schoolyard — dissipated the beginnings of a squabble between Claude Lemieux and the fat woman's child. Jay Pee Jodoin mentally heaved a sigh: This time he hadn't had to be a buffer.

"What're you doing here? Are you nuts! If you get caught...."

Linda Lauzon didn't even bother taking her finger out of her nose to reply.

"We won't get caught, there's nobody there. Hurry up, slowpokes, we can walk home together!"

And for the first time in years, three boys and three girls turned on to Gilford Street together to walk home from school. And as if to thumb their noses at the whole neighbourhood, even if they were fairly sure nobody would see them, they all put their arms around each other's waists, an attractive group of children fleeing the torments of school, and they walked down the street singing the Scouts' song, "Youkadee, youkaday."

The enchanted forest was really and truly dead for him now, and the fat woman's child sang a little louder than his friends as they walked past it.

The sun struck her full in the face, like a slap. Too much light all at once. Too much direct heat. The humidity was making her forehead sweat. She took shelter under the drugstore awning at the corner of Cartier and Mont-Royal and watched the passing strollers, glad to be offering their faces and arms to the caress of these first hours of summer they'd looked forward to for so long.

Across the street the Mont-Royal Convent stood imposingly on its pretentious lawns, the only islet of greenery on this street of concrete, the only manifestation of wealth in the surrounding poverty.

The sun fell over everything, convent, stores, the street, cars, passersby; it was too harsh, erasing colours, emphasizing people's ugliness, their lack of taste, their insignificance. Yes, that was it, their insignificance. She could have taken them one by one and beaten them, so insignificant did they seem to her. Like her mother with her fears and her complaints and her miserable little life. She hadn't seen her mother in broad daylight for a long time but she was convinced that if Albertine were here right now, at the corner of Cartier and Mont-Royal, she would strike her as even smaller, even more...insignificant. Why had that word kept coming to her for the past few minutes? Because she herself had just done something she thought was brave? Throwing that apron in Monsieur Dubé's face, giving the finger to the chef who'd been trying to get her into a corner for months, the urge that had come over her to grab that goddamn lamp and chuck it into the wall, that sentence uttered slowly like a threat — "Next time I come here I'll be a customer! And drunk!" — had all that given her the right to judge others, to feel superior to them? Yes! She had just taken an important step, made a choice that was going to change her life, give her wings, return her to the world where she belonged, once again she had taken her life in hand to shake it up, turn it around, once again she had incited fate while the rest of them, those passersby with their hesitant little steps, their evasive expressions, their ridiculous clothes, who had the grotesque look of consenting victims, needed only the presence of an oppressive sun to make themselves think they were happy!

She wanted to shake her fist at the sun and curse it, but she restrained herself. That's the kind of thing you do when you're drunk, at dawn, when that goddamn ball of fire dares to kill the night, not when you walk out of a Bar-B-Q on an empty stomach at four in the afternoon and you've just quit your job....

She merely spat on the ground and felt relieved. She was a nightbird and she only liked Mont-Royal and the other streets of Montreal when they were corseted with neon and nearly empty, at the hour when lawful businesses were closing up and the bars, taverns, nightclubs, blind pigs that flirted with the forbidden, the unclean, the indecent, were opening their doors to deceptive dreams that were usually false and often dangerous — but so comforting. She had always felt the need to console herself for living and the night had given her a balm or rather a drug that blunted her intelligence, her questioning, and now she was going back to it after a few months of unfaithfulness, and her relief was boundless.

She'd have gladly stayed there waiting for the sun to set rather than meet it head on, but there were four or five long hours of daylight left before night, and she didn't feel like being taken for a hooker. She smiled, though, at the image she was offering: A hooker at the door of a drugstore.... She crossed Cartier then, almost at a run, to seek out the beneficent shade of an old shoe store. She turned her head as she passed the office of Household Finance because she really owed them too much money and she was really taking too long to pay it off.

Where was she heading now? Certainly not home. Dorion Street in the poor part of town, the narrow passage between two houses, the inner courtyard, the miserable apartment at the back where once again she would be running into her husband, that despicable little man, twice a day: evenings when he was coming back from work as she was leaving, mornings when he was leaving and she was coming home, drunk, from some eventful party with other nightowls like herself; the iron bed inherited from her grandmother, the rickety wooden table, the fridge that was brand new and useless because no one ever ate in that house — it all upset her and she started trying to find some cool dark place where she could quietly wait for the dark. Something like a church, but without the smell of incense and the weight of religion, something like a tavern but where the women could sit with the men and prove they could lean against them any time. But everywhere, it was too bright.

She surprised herself thinking she should have put off her scene at the Bar-B-Q for a few hours to avoid braving the assaults of the sun.

After all, didn't she often boast about not seeing the daylight for a week and even longer in the winter-time?

She was thirsty.

"Before, when you used to sleep on top of me, you were too heavy. I could feel your weight. It was warm. You'd stretch out full length on my belly and rest your cold muzzle on my neck. And I'd scratch behind your ears because you'd told me that was where you most liked being scratched. Then you'd start up your little motor. Sometimes, never on purpose, your claws would go into my skin. It only hurt a little and I didn't complain. We'd stay like that for a long long time. You'd tell me you could hear my heart beating and I'd try to hear yours."

Two tears were running down his neck, tears he felt he'd shed long ago, days or even months before; tears that had taken months to bypass the wings of his nose, to cross his cheeks before they slowly rolled down his neck. He realized he had started to cry on the day he realized that Duplessis was being obliterated and that today was the day when everything would stop: His tears would stop flowing, his heart would stop beating for his cat, because he wouldn't exist any more, not even for him—the summer that had announced itself to him personally, that he'd thought was his own, time, life, the world. A locked door had signified to him the end of everything, and from now on he would be just an adolescent adrift in a world he didn't understand.

He had resumed his favourite position on the neighbours' verandah: lying on his back with his arms stretched out on either side, he had waited for Duplessis to finish grooming himself — even though he was no longer the amused witness he'd been in the past, he could sense when the little pink tongue would emerge from the cat's mouth to lick a paw that was now invisible — before he invited him to lie on his stomach. Duplessis had obeyed at once but Marcel felt nothing at first because his cat didn't weigh anything now. Only the whiskers tickling his neck, as cool, and moist as ever, indicated that his cat was still there. And the purring that had started up by itself. Marcel looked like a young crucifixion victim, palms open, feet crossed, waiting for everything to end.

Duplessis had said nothing yet. Marcel knew he was listening to him because he'd raised his head for a few seconds and seen the beautiful yellow eyes that watched over him lovingly whenever he'd been sick and when Rose, or Violette, or Mauve laid him on the living room sofa with a cool washcloth on his forehead. Human eyes that understood. Duplessis always waited till Marcel had reached the end of his grievances or his enthusiasms before he spoke. But this time Marcel wasn't too sure he was anxious for his cat to speak. Because his voice, that too, had been fading away for some time now. It was no longer a voice bursting with health, that swore readily, that was sharp when ruthlessness was called for, tender when a surprise was coming, or a gift, no, it was a tiny range of high-pitched notes that seemed to be produced by an imp with a cold; sometimes there were even parts missing, like parts of Duplessis' body. The long lessons about life or nature or the arts were impossible now because the essential ideas were lost between two tinklings of a tiny bell. Once, Duplessis even apologized for his perforated speech. And so Marcel had been unable to learn anything for months now, and his tears were flowing because his education had been so abruptly interrupted, for reasons he didn't comprehend but knew were perfectly unfair.

"Don't move. Keep your muzzle there. This may be the last time...."

Duplessis suddenly raised his astonished head. Marcel saw the muzzle, the whiskers, the beautiful eyes, the pointed ears suspended there.

"You think I don't know our time's nearly up? You think I can't read the signs? You showed me so much in the past ten years, you made me understand so many things, I can think by myself now, you know!"

He closed his arms as if he expected to find the soft fur, the muscles, the fat too, because in the late spring Duplessis was always slightly obese.

"You don't have a body now, Duplessis, you don't have a voice.... The door to the house is locked.... You're all rejecting me and I want to know why!"

Again, the damp presence of the muzzle on his neck. His heart melted.

"No, no, I don't want to know! I don't want it to happen! Stay with me, my love, we'll be so good for each other! Everything outside of you is evil, everything that's outside all of you scares me! Don't leave me!"

Behind him, a click. The door to the house had just opened wide. Wild with hope, he rolled over till he was flat on his stomach in front of the door. Duplessis' head was now level with his right ear. Beyond the doorway Marcel could see suitcases, dozens of suitcases piled up along the length of the hallway that led to the kitchen. Metal trunks with shiny, reinforced corners, huge open wicker baskets from which sleeves of blouses, hems of skirts, shoeboxes and hatboxes emerged. A dress from another age walked down the hallway. Rose, Violette, or Mauve. A shadow was carrying garments that would join others in a jumble that was surprising for these women who were normally so neat and tidy. They were pushing furniture, piling chairs, putting on slipcovers, taking down curtains. They were preparing for something urgent in the dimness inside this house, something horrible and final.

Marcel cried out, so loudly that the cat's head flattened against the floor of the balcony.

"You're all moving away!"

The adolescent could feel his whole life leave his body all at once, at the same time the air abruptly left his lungs. He spat out, he vomited the breath of knowledge he had been given by the women, by Duplessis, and he felt as empty and ignorant as when he had first met the five of them. Once again he was the lisping child from whom they had taken away and given back his love, in whom later on they'd deposited marvels; he was restored to that state of ignorance from which he'd started out and he thought, *I'm not thirteen years old any more, I'm just three...I'm fwee years old and I don't know nothing and my kittycat's gone away, my kitty's dead, the doggy killed him.... Help me.... We can start all over again if you want....*

The cat's warmth was next to his ear, the imp's high-pitched voice was expressing...what? Apologies? Justifications?

Marcel rolled onto his back and howled, howled like a wolf as his family used to do in the past, in the

200

country, when the pressure was too great and the words wouldn't come. An animal's cry. A tiny little wolf, a sick cub caught in a trap, was trying to gather up his remaining strength so as not to sink definitively into madness. Or death.

His mother's voice made him start and the three-year-old child imprisoned in the body of a boy of thirteen jumped to his feet.

Albertine was standing in front of the metal fence.

"What're you doing there lying on the gallery of a house nobody lives in! How many times, how many years have I been telling you not to go there! You want me to come and drag you away by the scruff of your neck once and for all, eh, is that what you want?"

And for the first time she pushed open the gateway to the marvellous. Marcel felt everything around him become hideously normal. Duplessis' head disappeared and the door closed behind him, while his mother crossed the front yard and climbed up the three steps. Her well-aimed slap made his ear ring. He got up, crouching to dodge the second clout that followed incredibly quickly, and ran out of the yard.

Albertine stood in the middle of the gallery, dumbfounded. She knew she was at the threshold of her son's madness, at the entrance to a forbidden world where you don't give birth to abnormal children because nothing is abnormal there, a world where her uncle Josaphat-le-violon had spent time, that had been undermining her son's life for ten years now. A world that should have been destroyed if anyone had known how to do so.

Driven by rage, she threw herself on the doorbell.

"Go away! Get out of here! Leave us alone! For God's sake leave us alone!"

As he turned the corner at Fabre and Gilford, Marcel fell into the net of the six children joyously coming home from school. Greeted by a volley of "Pigeon! Pigeon! Pigeon!," he was immediately surrounded, teased, tousled, and for once his cousin didn't defend him. He stood there with his head down, receiving pushes that weren't altogether friendly, and strident cries — almost unaware of what was going on, devastated as he was by his sense that he had just lost everything.

The fat woman's child wasn't taking part in his friends' cruel game but neither was he doing anything to break it up; he stood a little to one side, his hand on his chest as if he was witnessing some shattering event, his mouth half-open, head tilted to his shoulder. He knew he should have done what he usually did — throw himself into the fray, push away Jay Pee Jodoin first because he took every battle, even the most innocuous, very seriously, then stop Carmen Ouimet from pulling Marcel's hair too hard, while keeping an eye on Linda Lauzon's hands because she was quick with a slap. Instead, he stood there watching his cousin who stood a good head taller and could have hammered them if he'd wanted, because he had proved so often to him, the fat woman's child, how strong he was, but now he was letting himself be pounded by one after the other, without reacting.

After a little kick in the rear that was more humiliating than painful — a kick in the rear, even the flimsiest, is always humiliating — bestowed without conviction by Claude Lemieux though he was the most cowardly of them all, Marcel finally raised his eyes and looked at his cousin, as if he'd just regained consciousness after a long fainting spell.

Distress.

The fat woman's child had never seen anything like it. It was in the eyes, yes, and that broke your heart, but you could see it too on the shoulders, the arms, the arch of the back. It was like an aura of extreme fragility; it resembled a voiceless call for help, saying this is your last chance, your very last chance and afterwards it will be too late; it was a one-way bridge between them that Marcel could not cross. If he held out his hand Marcel wouldn't drown; but if he didn't move, it was all over.

The pushing and shouting were less enthusiastic, the game was already losing its edge. Carmen Brassard blew on a lock of hair that had fallen onto her face. Jay Pee Jodoin was barely shouting. Claude Lemieux had taken refuge behind a tree after he'd delivered his kick... Did they sense what was going on, or were they already tired of this game with an overly passive adversary?

Silence fell as the two cousins stood face to face.

The fat woman's child thought to himself that after the day that had just passed he could never be altogether sincere with Marcel because he had intended to abandon him, out of sheer jealousy, and now he was ashamed of himself; but a nearly irresistible burst of affection that sprang from a single glance, the most hopeless, most helpless of gazes, urged him to go to his cousin. He wished he could throw himself on him, kiss him on the stomach, the face, the mouth, dust off his back, his buttocks, the back of his head to erase the kicks and slaps Marcel had just been subjected to. He wished he could have earned his cousin's forgiveness by cleansing him of the humiliations, of all the humiliations in his life.

He had just discovered jealousy and lying, but something else, something new that wasn't pity, that was at once loftier and greater than pity and that he did not yet understand, presented itself to him, and he had absolutely no idea what to do with it. When tenderness is joined with pity, what are you supposed to do?

The five other children had stepped back slightly, realizing that something very important was happening. They were breathing hard, winded, looking now at one of the cousins, now at the other. Were they going to kill one another or make permanent peace? Seeing himself having to put up with Marcel all day and all summer long, Jay Pee Jodoin hoped the fat woman's child was going to settle his hash once and for all.

But he was disappointed. They all were. Especially the fat woman's child, who felt unable to do what he wanted to do.

With a hint of a smile that he hoped looked sincere, encouraging without being condescending, he brought up his hand and waved it like someone saying a sad good-bye. Marcel understood and lowered his eyes. It would have taken nothing more than a forefinger on the tip of his nose, a hand pushing back his hair, perhaps even just a shoulder brushing against his chest. The contact wasn't made. Because of shyness.

Distress. Shyness.

As soon as he'd turned the corner, the fat woman's child felt cowardly, naked, and for the second time that day, unworthy.

Across the lane his aunt was screaming at the top of her lungs as she climbed up the stairs of their house.

"Couldn't you wait till you were inside before you started yelling your head off..."

The fat woman was sipping a Coke through two straws. Between mouthfuls of the sugary liquid that she allowed to fizz in her mouth before she swallowed, she set the bottle on the armrest and watched Fabre Street, nearly devoid of people at this time of day but full of little details — passing cars; birds flying from tree to tree; a sneaky cat trying to hide in the grass that was already high, head raised towards the lowest branches where those delicious sparrows often perch; Marie-Sylvia pulling her rocking chair onto the sidewalk because she knows she won't have any customers till the children come home from school, and who rocks at a ridiculous speed, as if she was leading a rocking-chair race; the play of the sun in the highest branches of the trees — trivial details, but ones she liked to watch while she slowly rocked. Friday night supper would be fixed quickly, she was alone in the house, so why not treat herself to a little hour on the balcony? To Madame Guérin who was walking by with too much rouge on her cheeks, or to Monsieur L'Heureux on his way home from church where he spent a good part of his days licking the curé's ass as people were so quick to say about him, she would offer a polite Bonjour, without encouraging conversation. She wanted this hour for herself, before the family invaded the house like an army: Albertine home from Schiller's, Gabriel exhausted from the week, whose silence would weigh more heavily than his sister's babbling, her three famished sons complaining because it was Friday when the only things they were allowed to eat were tasteless, Marcel who had left the house a lunatic and would come home to eat unhinged, as usual.

She was rarely alone and she cherished these brief moments when she could choose for herself what she was going to do: in the winter it was usually a book she'd devour while sitting in front of the silent radio, in summer a quick trip to balconville, slowly rocking and sipping a Coke — though it was never cold enough for her liking because she sipped it rather than downing it in two gulps like her sister-in-law.

A book lay next to her chair, the latest novel by Gabrielle Roy which she hadn't read yet and had brought out just in case.... But no urge to read had struck her during the splendor of this late afternoon. Plunged in the cool shadow of the balcony she had decided she needed only some little nothings that made her feel secure: summer had truly arrived and she intended to spend it out here, watching it unfurl its charms.

And so she had witnessed the scene between Albertine and Marcel; she had even craned her neck a little and seen out of the corner of her eye, between two steps of the outside staircase, her sister-in-law's visit to the neighbours' gallery. She had heard her pleading and, ill at ease, she'd wanted to go inside, to hide in the bedroom so Albertine wouldn't suspect anything. To pretend, as usual. But Albertine had left the front yard too quickly and had noticed her right away and had taken her to task not only for what had just happened but for the whole day, the month, the year, her life. That too was as usual. Albertine had climbed the stairs shrieking incoherently things her sister-in-law could easily make out because they were always the same. The names of Thérèse and Marcel kept recurring, followed by oaths — when Albertine undressed an altar she left it totally bare for a long time — and curses.

And faced with the obvious injustice of some of her sister-in-law's remarks about her children, she hadn't been able to restrain herself and had reproached her for the way she'd just treated Marcel.

Albertine stopped in front of what had for a long time been her mother's bedroom window, a very small sash window, narrow and surrounded by a frieze of paler bricks, and rested one hand against it.

"I didn't say a quarter of what he deserved..."

The six children arrived in front of the house, looking up towards this woman who was so unpredictable, who frightened them all because she was liable to blow up anywhere, any time — they had seen her at Soucis' throw a slice of calf's liver in the owner's face because it wasn't to her liking, shower insults at Marie-Sylvia because the price of Mell-O-Rolls was up one cent, chase Monsieur L'Heureux down the block because he had dared to call Marcel "pigeon" in front of her — at once excited and worried to see her transformed into a fury before their eyes again.

The fat woman's child was standing to one side. He didn't want his mother to get involved publicly in one of his aunt's tantrums, and vowed that if she started yelling again he'd run away... To join Marcel in his enchanted forest? Up to Mont-Royal to get lost in the noise of the street? Into the lane, under a gallery with the stray cats and all those things that swarm in the dark?

But when Albertine started talking he stood paralyzed under the little maple tree, as he had been before Marcel's secrets that morning. The same sense of poorly formulated urgency, the same magma of badly-knit words that clash and jostle as long as the mouth that speaks them cannot stem the tide, descended from the balcony in intermittent waves, and he couldn't stop himself from stepping closer to the house, grabbing hold of the wrought-iron fence still warm from the sun's caresses, and straining his ear toward his aunt's tremendous suffering.

All at once Albertine fell silent and it seemed as if it was over, that she was going to disappear into the house.

But the scene that followed surprised everyone.

Albertine looked up, stared at her sister-in-law for several seconds, her expression like that of a religious fanatic unsure of where she is, then she turned her head towards the street. Her reason seemed restored and she brought her hand to her forehead. She crossed the balcony, walking around the fat woman's rocking chair, and leaned against the railing. She stood there perfectly straight, hands flat on the varnished wood, head high — a rare posture for her. And when she opened her mouth everything became clear.

It began as a barely murmured recitative, to set the stage; it was about life in general and about a personal cage in particular; about ordeals repressed in the hollow of a bed, a pillow over her head so the rest of the house wouldn't hear the cries of rage; about lack of privacy, hypocrisies, loves that cannot be expressed and white sauce that congeals on your plate; it was about loneliness in the midst of unending activity, and madness furtively glimpsed when nothing else is left — the solution for everything, the perfect refuge. It was slow and precise and gently modulated, and it broke your heart.

Then came the grand aria.

The set represented a three-storey brown brick house with three superimposed balconies and a staircase that went from the street up to the second floor. On the middle balcony were two women. The confidante was a fat woman in a rocking chair who merely nodded assent to everything the other one sang, not daring to interrupt or make a comment; the heroine, the tragic heroine, was a plain little woman in a polkadot dress who was expressing herself clearly for perhaps the first time in her life. Her song rippled gently without ever rising very high; instead it seemed to descend towards the chorus, six children to whose backs this lament was not really being addressed but who just happened to be there when the scene began — as if such a thing as coincidence existed. Exactly ten years earlier their mothers, pregnant then, had sung "Le temps des cerises" on this same balcony, in a moment of communion unique in their lives. Then, the fat woman had not been relegated to the role of confidante; she had been the soloist in a chorus filled with hope that had risen straight up in the night over Fabre Street.

But this new aria, which was terribly perfect and was sent up from that same balcony by a woman who had not been part of that chorus filled with hope, was concerned exclusively with two children: a brainless girl, heartless and lacking a conscience, and a useless boy, the two poles of a tragedy, two causes of a crucifixion. It was a song of rare economy, closer to Gregorian chant than to the romantic, and the six children folded their arms across their chests to collect their thoughts, and to keep themselves from crying.

As the song unfolded, doors opened along Fabre Street. The mothers of other children, older or younger ones, came out on their balconies and they in turn leaned against the railing or the supporting column. They punctuated the heroine's grand aria with onomatopoeia or with snatches of sentences that wrapped themselves around the song and carried it higher. You could hear exclamations of "Oh, yes!" or "That's for sure!" or "Isn't it the truth!" or "You're so right!" that underlined the ingratitude of children, their thoughtlessness and their demands. Their own misfortunes were less flamboyant that those of the little woman on the balcony, but they identified with the one who had dared to speak out even though the heroine didn't know they were there. Their bodies swayed to the melody, some of them humming along with their mouths closed, others letting out little moans that brought them relief. More voices were added to the voices, the song finally took flight, and it rose directly up into the incredibly blue sky.

The aria ended in a whisper, in a long drawn-out note terminating in a sigh after the tragic singer had insinuated that beneath it all there lay smoldering a great love that could never be expressed. She was leaning over the railing in a position of extreme weakness. She stayed that way, without straightening up, as if she were expecting a tremendous ovation that was long in coming.

The chorus dispersed. Slowly the children walked away to join their mothers. Only the fat woman's child stayed at the foot of the stairs. He dared not even go up to the altar of the tragedy.

The confidante rose, bent over the tragic singer and took her by the hand, making her straighten up until finally she came and leaned against her shoulder. The confidante said a single phrase that no one else could hear because it was murmured into the ear of the tragic one. They went into the house as if exiting a stage.

The fat woman's child clapped his hands, one against the other, three times.

With his knees in the damp earth, sitting on his heels, head lowered and arms crossed in deep contemplation, he gazed at his collapse with a coolness that surprised him. The first time he'd come to the enchanted forest he had wanted to cry out in rage, to roll on the ground, to kick himself as he'd done so often if his mother yelled at him too much when he was little, but he hadn't had the strength, and now even his appetite for it had vanished.

He reviewed his day, went through it step by step — the misleading promises of the summer that was pretending to offer itself to him, his confessions to his cousin, his first epileptic seizure in front of somebody outside the family, his dream of Duhamel, his aunt's incomprehension though she wanted so much to be understanding, his erection in his mother's bed, his discovery of the definitive loss of Duplessis and the departure of Rose, Violette, Mauve and their mother, Florence — and he thought he was very naïve. Yet he'd known for a long time that such a day would come eventually; he'd known ever since the first holes started appearing in Duplessis, since the first doubting looks from the women next door — because they doubted him, he was sure of that. He knew but didn't want to know: the future had to resemble the ten years just passed because more and more, he felt the need to take refuge next door with his friends, to listen to Duplessis speak; but he knew that too, and didn't want to know, for hadn't these hours, these great swathes of days spent wandering from room to room, become in fact *inactive*, a mere pastime, a consolation for the things that hurt too much? How long had it been since he'd practised the piano? Since he'd picked up a book to devour, or a pencil to write? The summer before he had played the huge piano in that hall of wonders that transported him so high he'd thought he could never come down again... What had he done all winter, all spring? He had listened to Florence play, delighted, yes, often transported even, but it was different because he had simply experienced the delight of someone else. He hadn't even followed the piece as he listened, trying to play it on an imaginary keyboard the way the women had shown him...

In the past, after an impassioned speech by Duplessis, he used to throw himself into some activity, no matter which, the first one that presented itself; he worked, he learned, he slogged away, and then he would come out of it exhausted, ecstatic, and richer, always richer by something, and more and more so because he liked to work and to feel he was improving himself and could boast about it. But for almost a year now he'd been nothing more than a spectator, a little like the lisping, ignorant three-year-old who had come one day to deposit his dying cat in the front yard. He had lost his passion for learning and creating, and now he was gazing at that loss, which had been condensed into a single day, as the illustration of this period in his life that was ending, with a frightening chill.

214

He opened his eyes, looked around him. The sun had long since stopped playing in the dense foliage of the bleeding hearts. He saw the blue of the sky through the branches because the sun was still high, but the light on the leaves was uniform, painted there by a child who has not yet grasped the subtleties of the colour green.

And then he began not to pick the bleeding hearts, but to tear them off one by one, taking care to crush them all between his thumb and forefinger. They burst, pink insects with no juice, and immediately took on a darker colour, closer to red, as Marcel rolled them between his fingers, reducing them to a moist, vaguely sickening paste that he proceeded to throw over his shoulder. He would look closely at a flower, grab it by the thread that held it to the branch, conscientiously crush it, and throw it away. It took a long time because there were a lot of flowers.

Where there wasn't a single one left he thought the enchanted forest looked very bare, as it would in July when the flowers fall, and he wished he could put them back. He had anticipated the end of the bleeding hearts and now he wanted to do the same thing to the whole enchanted forest. And to everything it represented.

If the old lady who lived at 1474 Gilford had come out of her house just then she'd have been very surprised to suddenly see her grove of bleeding hearts start writhing where it stood. Like an epileptic child with no one to help him through a seizure.

Supper was gloomy and silent. The fat woman had warned her husband, Gabriel, and her two older sons, Richard and Philippe, that Albertine was having one of her bad days, so they didn't dare let their hair down as they often did on Friday night, after a week of work. They had taken their places at the table, watching Albertine out of the corner of an eye. She had stayed in her mother's rocking chair, hunched over the radio that was broadcasting French *chansonettes* and it was hard to say if they were helping her or not, because her face gave nothing away.

She had turned down her sister-in-law's suggestion that she go to bed, preferring to take refuge in this corner of the dining room that over the years had become the shelter for any family members who wanted to withdraw for one reason or another. It was an odd choice because the dining room was the nerve centre of the house: located at the heart of the apartment, it was the busiest place, the liveliest, the setting for family get-togethers and a fair number of their fights. And it was absolutely impossible to feel really alone there, especially since the old rocking chair that sat diagonally in front of the enormous radio dominating one corner of the room almost touched the table where the household gathered for their evening meal.

And since every crisis tended to occur around six o'clock, because that was the only moment in the day when all the members of both families were there together — there were four sittings for breakfast: first Gabriel alone, since he started work very early, then Philippe and Richard, who started at nine, then the children on their way to school and finally, after everyone else had left, the two women of the house — they had often eaten supper while watching Marcel rocking too hard after a battle with his mother, or Albertine herself who reacted badly to any criticism of her culinary skills and could stop serving in the middle of the meal if she heard the slightest grunt of dissatisfaction, or the fat woman's child protesting because he wasn't allowed to go to a movie at the Passe-Temps by himself and declared he was going on a hunger strike, or Thérèse, especially Thérèse before she got married, when she'd flare up over nothing, fling herself into the rocking chair, turn up the radio and for long minutes howl along with Johnny Ray or Frank Sinatra while the rest of the family kept their noses in their plates and dared not make a single remark because that would have set off absolute pandemonium.

Sulking in front of everyone like that made the rest of the family feel guilty, something that happened often in this house.

The fat woman's child was sitting on the other side of the table. He could see his aunt in profile looking very withdrawn, suddenly aged, almost weak — Albertine, the family terror. Others said she was becoming more and more like her mother, Victoire, who had run the house with consummate skill for years and then towards the end of her life had given up every battle and taken refuge in front of her radio, content to mutter insults aimed at no one in particular and everyone in general. In fact, Albertine was more and more often withdrawing into a corner of the dining room, even abandoning the household chores to her sister-in-law, except during brief periods of agitation as she'd done for the ironing this afternoon when she'd launched into some domestic activity to numb herself, or to forget.

But he was puzzled by this immobility of his aunt's, by her prostration after her lyrical flight on the balcony. Something was brewing. She was going to tell them some news that would stun them all. Or do something irrevocable. He was afraid for Marcel who he knew was lying low in that scrap of front lawn he'd transformed into an enchanted forest; he had a vision of this woman driven into the labyrinth of madness and beating up on her child even though he could have sent her flying with one swipe of his arm. That was when he became aware of something that made him drop his knife and fork onto the table. It was not Marcel who was in danger, it was all of them.

Albertine turned to him abruptly. Had she guessed what he was thinking? She looked at him for several seconds, then said:

"Do you smell something burning?"

The fat woman ran to the kitchen and came back, visibly relieved.

"No, no, it's all right. Everything's turned off."

Albertine continued to stare at her nephew.

"Where's Marcel?"

He picked up his knife and fork, cut a small piece of fish and brought it to his mouth.

"Answer me when I speak to you!"

Was he going to betray his cousin's hiding place? Was he going to get up and take his aunt to Gilford Street, show her the most beautiful place in the world, the most magical invention, saying, That's where he is, that's where it happens, jump on him before he destroys us all? And what if he was mistaken after all? If it was Albertine who risked annihilating her son, as he'd thought at first?

"Don't ask me where he is. I'm not his guardian angel."

He turned and looked in the direction of the window. Stretched out on the balcony railing, Peter Pan, also in profile, was playing his pipe.

Marie-Sylvia watched Marcel cross the street. He seemed to be on his way home. He'd sworn it was his mother who had sent him and she hadn't bothered calling Albertine, whom she spoke to as little as possible in any case. She was always terrified to see Marcel's mother come into her store; she was a difficult customer and her moods were frightening: Albertine would curtly ask for what she wanted, Marie-Sylvia would put the goods on the counter without a word, pick up the money, and the two women would take their leave of one another without even a thank you. And that was when things were going well. But when Albertine decided something didn't suit her, that the Coke wasn't cold enough or the surprise packages not full enough...

Ever since the scene that afternoon when Albertine had exposed her pain to all the women in the neighbourhood, Marie-Sylvia saw her neighbour in a different way. Not yet with sympathy, it was too embryonic, but now she suspected that between the cold woman she was on her good days and the fury of her bad ones there was another — the real one — whom life had broken and who now concealed herself beneath a character she tried to make aggressive so the others would leave her in peace. The suffering she had sensed in Albertine was incomparably pure and Marie-Sylvia felt that she herself had grown for having witnessed such a tragic scene. If anyone had intimated during all those years that one day this woman would touch the very depths of her soul, she would have laughed. She had always thought Albertine had been born with nothing going for her, and that she'd die without even realizing it.

She walked towards the broom closet, rubbing her back. The sidewalk had to be swept again before she went to bed. Nowadays she waited till it was dark, to avoid the sarcasm of the families who'd come out on their balconies to enjoy a little cool air. Despite this clumsy trick she couldn't avoid the barely hidden laughter of those who could hear her broom stirring up the dust. That they called her a witch didn't bother her — people respect witches because they're afraid of them — but for them to think she was an idiot.... What's idiotic about keeping your own sidewalk clean?

She switched off all her lights, descended the two steps and started fervently sweeping despite the pain in her back. A shape — Marcel, round-shouldered and with that waddle he'd had since childhood — was standing in front of the house next door to his, that empty house she'd often seen him furtively emerge from, excited as a flea and talking to himself. He seemed reluctant to push open the metal gate in the fence around the front yard. Perhaps he was afraid of what was in store for him...or of what he was about to do.

And all at once Marie-Sylvia knew that in years to come she would be known in the annals of Plateau Mont-Royal as the woman who had sold Marcel the matches.

For the first time in ages she didn't finish sweeping her sidewalk but went inside to hide at the back of her shop. Ten years earlier, Marcel had stolen her cat; now he was about to steal her reputation.

He tossed into the sewer in the LaMennais lane the brown bag where Marie-Sylvia had concealed the Eddy matches. He brought the blue-and-white box to his nose. A pungent smell. He felt a little calmer.

At home he wasn't allowed to touch matches — as if he was still a child! —which infuriated him. Often, when his mother and his aunt weren't there, he would go to the tin box hanging on the wall where they kept the matches, steal a few, and take them out to the shed or the lane. But he didn't waste them right away like the other children in the neighbourhood, whom he'd sometimes seen under the galleries, burning old papers or trying to light cigarettes that would make them sick: First he steeped his fingers in the sharp, faintly nauseating smell of sulphur, stuck his nose in between his joined hands, closed his eyes and took a long, deep breath.

The odour was like the gates of Hell. He had heard a priest say from the pulpit one Sunday morning that when a sinner arrived at the gates of Hell, he'd smell the brimstone before he smelled the fire. He had added: "If ever you're tempted to commit a mortal sin, open a box of matches, bring it up to your nose, and smell what's in store for you at the gates of Hell!" That day the entire parish had gone to the threshold of eternal damnation, and for a while their sins were not so numerous.

But Marcel, though he was the most terrified of them all, had often returned to that smell, the way you keep pressing your finger on a sore to see if it's still there, still hurting. The acrid perfume frightened him but it attracted him too: He knew that with one of these flimsy little sticks you could set off a calamity, and while that terrified him, it reassured him too. Some day when things were going badly, when he was the unhappiest child in the world, when he couldn't help himself, he was going to take one of these bits of wood soaked in sulphur and set off an irreparable disaster, a fire, fire in his own life and in the lives of the others, fire that would purify everything. And then the world, his world, could begin again.

At night, to put himself back to sleep after his four a.m. pee, he imagined the flickering flame coming close to the wooden fence around the school, to his own varnished desk, his teacher's soutane and most of all to his mother's hair. Hair comes from the brain, hair is an emanation of the brain, if you set fire to a person's hair that person might make a fresh start, become like a new person, a child, a baby...and what he wanted more than anything was for his mother to make a fresh start.

But never in his wildest fantasies had the flames been headed for the house where Rose, Violette, Mauve, and their mother Florence lived. Because that house had been his first haven before the invention of the enchanted forest. It was from that first shelter that he'd drawn the strength to create the second.

Now he was gazing at that dwelling for the last time, his nose still in between his hands as he shifted from foot to foot the way he liked to do. That was where he had been the happiest, but his happiness was ending now, and that was where he was going to start a fire.

He knew they wouldn't insult him now by locking the door. And so he pushed it with one hand, leaving the first trace of sulphur on the glass.

Suitcases, crates, and cardboard boxes were piled in the hallway. There were dustcovers on all the living room furniture. The piano had been shifted and for the first time the lid was closed. The key had even been taken out to indicate that everything — the music as much as the rest — really was finished now. No more pictures on the walls, just pale rectangles that revealed the wallpaper's true colours. There was a smell of dust that had been stirred up, of old things left behind in corners that had now been disturbed, of the mustiness of cloth folded away in the backs of cupboards for too long, of mothballs that had perhaps protected some raccoon cap from another time.

In the rounded recess in the hallway where a coal stove used to stand, that had heated the whole house through a network of pipes in the ceiling, lay a huge red tapestry travelling bag that he recognized right away; all the treasures of his life, everything he'd learned, had come from that bag: books, never the same and always fascinating, music scores he'd learned to decipher at an amazing speed, paper to write on, paper to draw on, brushes and poster-paints — and Duplessis himself who often slept there. If he knelt down in front of this bag, if he opened it, the past ten years of his life would spring out all at once and he would die. He hesitated. To die himself, or to cause death. He sat on the bag, holding the box of matches against his heart.

225

Life without them, without *him* would be impossible, but dying scared him. Because of the gates of Hell and what was beyond them, which worried him a lot more than the smell of brimstone. To go away with them, with him? Beg them to keep him, to erase him from the world too, to take him wherever they were going, which certainly wasn't the gates of Hell? After all, what would be left for him after they had gone? He had just demolished the enchanted forest and now he was all alone, with no Duplessis, in a world that had rejected him.

A nearly transparent shadow walked past him. Mauve, carrying a pile of clothes, appeared not to see him. They too were being erased. Perhaps they couldn't see him now at all. He had ceased to exist for them. He crossed his arms and doubled over. The pain of rejection was so intense, he thought surely the fires of Hell couldn't be so terrible. And he decided to talk to them, to the women. In case they could still hear him.

"I let you down. Isn't that what it is? You tried to do something with me that I didn't understand and I wasn't up to your plans. But you never said what you wanted from me! You gave me things that were so beautiful I wanted to show everybody, but you told me to wait. You always told me to wait. To keep it all to myself. Not to show anything. But what were we waiting for? For me to be ready? Ready for what? For what? All those things you gave me, other people don't understand anyway! Why have such beautiful things and not be able to share them? I live my life all by myself and when I leave here I'm the only one who knows what it is I know! When I show little bits, my mother says she's going to lock me up! Does that mean I've got things inside that I can't ever take out, can't ever show? I don't want things that are just for me, that nobody else knows about! I don't want to go on living all by myself because I'm different from the others! Why play the piano only here? Why write only here? I want to be able to do it all everywhere, without people thinking I'm crazy!"

He stood up and started running through the house. But he never really ran into Rose, Violette, Mauve, or their mother Florence. He would see the edge of a skirt disappear through a doorway, but when he chased after it he'd find nothing but metal or cardboard trunks, open or closed, in rooms that were all topsy turvy. Then he understood that no explanations were ever going to come because Rose, Violette, Mauve, and their mother Florence might know nothing more about it than he did. They were there to give, to transmit, they had often done so through Duplessis, his great love, his mentor...and he'd let them down. And now they were going away because there was nothing more to be done with him. And so this was all his fault.

Suddenly he knelt down in the hallway, in front of the suitcase that contained all the treasures of his life, and he began striking his chest.

"It's all my fault, I know it is, but don't leave me here all alone. At least let me have Duplessis! Not just one of his ears and one eye and his muzzle, let me have all of him. Duplessis like he was when he was happy and we'd laugh together for hours.... Make him come back like you gave him back to me after he died. And I promise I'll never come here again when you're gone and I'll never talk about you. Or about him either. I swear I'll keep him for the rest of my life and I'll never ever talk about him.... Let me...just let me pet my...my cat...till the end of my days. That's all I ask. You can take back everything else."

He hadn't heard them come. All four women were standing around him now, so beautiful, so gentle. But all four had a helpless look that told him he would never again see even the tip of one of Duplessis' ears. This really was the end of everything. The ceremony that marked the end of everything. The final farewells.

He didn't know if they could hear him but he shouted at the top of his lungs.

"It's okay! Never mind! If I decide that Duplessis's still here nobody can stop me!"

Slowly he bent down, picked up the matches, held the box at arm's length for a few seconds, opened it, filled his lungs with the smell of sulphur.

"Here, Duplessis, come here my love.... We're going to start all over again.... The two of us. Just the two of us and nobody else."

The little stick of wood cracked and ignited at once. Marcel stuffed the cardboard box into a fold of the red tapestry suitcase and tossed the flaming match inside.

A wonderful explosion. With a strong smell of purifying sulphur. Marcel's face took on a pinkish hue, the way your face does when you come too close to a fire.

And when he turned back to Rose, Violette, Mauve, and their mother Florence, he was holding Duplessis in his arms.

In Violette's hands was a shapeless and unfinished piece of knitting. She made a brief remark that he couldn't hear but was able to read on her lips.

"What's been knitted is knitted, even if it's knitted badly."

He smiled.

"It doesn't matter. Fire destroys knitting too."

Thin smoke was beginning to rise out of Marcel's past.

Fabre Street was plunged in inky darkness. The street-lamp at the corner of the lane that usually daubed the fronts of houses with amber had been turned off. The nighthawks had left the sky after their daily nuptials and their harrowing cries could no longer be heard. A gentle breeze ruffled the trees now and then. It was a fine evening for a purifying fire.

Marcel came out of the house, holding Duplessis tight against him.

"We don't need them, you'll see. We can make our lives all by ourselves...."

Duplessis made no reply. Marcel hadn't yet realized that his cat no longer spoke, was no longer looking at him with those eyes — so intelligent, so full of mischief — with that grin as well, that the little boy used to call his sneery face, and that he often tried to imitate. Marcel did not yet know that Duplessis was now just an ordinary cat. Imaginary, but ordinary. He would frisk about like a cat, he'd rub up against his master's legs, demand to sleep in his bed, on his pillow, he'd have fits when he was hungry, he'd mark his territory because he hadn't been operated on, but he would no longer talk, no knowledge would come from him any more, no flash of humour, no declaration of love. He would be nothing more than the cat of a madman who thinks he has a cat.

Marcel jumped when he saw the shadow slowly rocking on the balcony. He knew it was Thérèse from the lily-of-the-valley perfume she sprayed on herself ten times a day, mixed with the reek of hastily gulped gin, and from the eternal cigarette swaying gently in rhythm with the rocking chair. She'd been watching him come up the stairs.

"Why're you always bent over like that! You walk like that, you climb the stairs like that...as if you're always looking for quarters! Don't you ever want to look up?"

Marcel sat down at her feet, discreetly setting Duplessis on the balcony floor. But the cat jumped right onto his knees, purring.

"When I feel like looking up I lie on my back!"

Thérèse laughed and memories of his childhood rose to Marcel's head so he had to lean against the prickly brick to keep from suffocating: Parc Lafontaine, the swing that was too high, the sandbox full of stray cats' turds, hiding in the mysterious bushes where the older children would go to celebrate some repugnant, incomprehensible ceremony, the whirligig that made you dizzy, the ladders that gave you vertigo, the sunsets when you were walking home late along Fabre Street and a spanking was waiting for you before a delicious meal because everyone had been worried and Albertine had nearly called the police three times, or so the fat woman said....

Peace. The beginning. All that was going to return. After the purification.

"You don't have much to say for yourself."

Thérèse had just mashed her cigarette under her left foot. Marcel thought that when his mother found the butt the next morning she'd know Thérèse had come here to smoke it practically under her nose, just to annoy her.

"You don't either."

A little wind. The leaves stir. Duplessis opens one eye, replaces his muzzle under his tail.

"Why'd you come here now? You haven't been here for ages."

Thérèse was already lighting another cigarette. Her brother smiled when the match cracked.

"I came to sit and rock for a while before I go to bed."

"Coming inside?"

"Never! I saw her once today, that'll do me for a month. For the summer. For the whole year."

They laughed. Together. The same three notes. As they used to.

"Haven't you got a rocking chair at your place?"

Thérèse shrugged and let out an oath before she spoke.

"What I've got at my place, kid, is a disease called being bored to death. My rocking chair's boring. Everything around me's boring. And if I don't get the hell out of there I'm going to die."

He could see her a little more clearly in the dark. He sensed the hesitation in her gestures, her head nodding not like someone falling asleep but like a drunk who can't control all the muscles in his neck.

"You're bombed...."

"Always."

He set his cat on the floor and stood up.

"You used to rock me in that chair when I was little...."

"Yes. And you'd go to sleep. And you were too heavy. And I loved you too much to wake you up."

He looked down, ran his index finger along the edge of the armrest.

"D'you still love me now?"

She smiled and the whole street lit up as if there were fireworks, when the big final rocket explodes and paints a look of rapture on every face.

"Anyhow, not so much I wouldn't wake you up if you got too heavy."

He was in her arms. He hadn't done this for years. He was too big now, he had to bend down to rest his head against his sister's neck, right there where the smell was strongest.

"You smell too. Like matches. Have you started smoking?"

No reply. Was he asleep already?

She started rocking very slowly, even though his legs dragged on the floor, and all at once she remembered the song of Tino Rossi's he used to like so much when he was little; the idiotic refrain she distorted for him, that made him laugh but amazingly put him to sleep as well: "Marinellaaaaa, your feet stink and your breath smells too..."

He laughed.

"Aren't you asleep?"

"You sing too flat."

A little tap on the rear. Like in the past. They both had a lump in their throats.

"This is the last time I'll rock you."

"It's the last time I'll ask you to...."

Their joy at pretending to squabble.

"How about that cat of yours? Where's your goddamn cat?"

Marcel smiled into his sister's neck, where it smelled of lily-of-the-valley.

"What cat?"

Nearby, a big tiger-striped tomcat dreamed he was listening to an adorable little boy play a baffling piano sonata with stupefying ease.

And already the smell of smoke was swirling along Fabre Street.

EPILOGUE

The ascent was relatively easy: up the outside staircase to the shed behind Monsieur L'Heureux's house after crossing the yard full of car skeletons, lawn mowers and empty oilcans, then take an old long strip of metal and open the latch in the wooden door, ascend the spiral staircase to the top floor and then climb the wobbly, rotten ladder to the roof. The trapdoor was easy to lift and all summer it opened directly onto the Big Dipper. You overlooked the whole of Fabre Street then, you felt powerful, you could see without being seen, you could even scare the whole neighbourhood by howling like a wolf or laughing like a vampire.

The descent was riskier: It was very dark in Monsieur L'Heureux's shed and just leaning over the trap-door made your head swim. The bottom rung of the ladder seemed beyond your reach, you had to hold the edge of the roof very tight with both hands, spread your legs, grope with your right foot for something to rest on, then let yourself drop down.... Climbing up towards the starry sky made you forget about spiders, mice, and other creepy crawlies, imaginary or not, but climbing *down* in the dark, not knowing where you were putting your foot or your hand, was torture, and few children could endure it.

That's why he was nearly always alone when he climbed up there.

He lay on his back on the sharp gravel, hands folded behind his head. He was thinking about Marcel who had shown him this hiding place out in the open one day but had never come up here with him since then, Marcel who'd been found fast asleep in Thérèse's arms a little earlier when the whole street had gone crazy because of the smoke, and his sister had tucked him in while the firemen were bashing in the door of the neighbours' house.

Inside, they found nothing. An empty house, abandoned for years but strangely clean: not a trace of dampness on the walls, no dust, the old stove and the sinks sparkling clean as if the inhabitants had just left after doing a massive housecleaning. In the recess in the hallway a box of Eddy matches had been almost consumed and a few floorboards had caught fire. They brought it under control in minutes, the fear had left Fabre Street, everyone had gone home to bed feeling at once reassured and anxious, reassured because the firemen had acted quickly, but anxious because fire, goddamn fire, was liable to break out at any time, anywhere, in these poorly protected houses of brick and wood.

Thérèse had disappeared through the back door and Albertine hadn't been able to chew her out as she'd have liked.

And Marcel had continued sleeping the sleep of the just.

The fat woman's child stood up, approached the edge of the roof, leaned over the void. Not a sound. Not a single movement. Everything was asleep, objects as well as humans. And he was watching. He could have named every inhabitant of every apartment in every one of the houses he looked down on; he could have imagined the positions of their bodies in their beds, the colour of their dreams, the way they smelled, especially his friends to whom he was preparing to recount all summer long a never-ending story that would mix together everything he knew: their daily lives, his own family's, the movies he had seen, the books he'd read, the radio programmes he'd listened to when his parents thought he was asleep — and Marcel's genius that he was about to plunder.

That story would have as its hero a little boy and a cat in an enchanted forest and they would believe it because now he knew how to lie, and he was that little boy.

A crystalline laugh, the sound of air displaced by something moving quickly. Peter Pan came and sat down beside him.

"Quite a day, eh?"

The fat woman's child tilted his head towards his left shoulder.

"You usually only come when I need you...."

"You want me to leave?"

"No, probably I was just thinking I needed you without knowing."

"Roofs are high, it's dangerous up here."

"Come off it.... I'm here every night in the summer and I've never seen you...."

Peter Pan came closer, draped one arm around the little boy's shoulders.

"Don't be a hypocrite, you know very well it's you who decides about everything I do. If I'm here it's because you called me, because you needed an arm around your shoulders. And when I leave in a little while, it'll mean you want that too."

The fat woman's child smiled sadly.

"Will you always be there?"

"No. You'll stop needing to go through me and you'll forget me."

"Forget you? Never!"

Peter Pan kneaded the boy's shoulders for a while.

"No promises. No oaths. Children are all alike, if you only knew.... Let's just enjoy what's up above our heads instead of talking nonsense."

And then they said nothing more.

Their feet were swinging in space, their heads were lost in the sky. The Little Dipper was turning around her mother, Mars was sparkling softly, Venus, most brilliant of all the planets, was showing off her beauty.

And the first quarter of the moon, the commencement of everything, the eternal new beginning, was sailing across it all as if on a starry pond.

In the hollow of the crescent moon lay a little boy with his arms behind his head and his legs crossed; he seemed to be dreaming; and at the end, hooked on by the collar of his shirt that might tear at any moment, dangled an adolescent.

Outremont, September 3, 1987 — June 15, 1989